Emily Butler

WITH PICTURES BY
Jennifer Thermes

CROWN BOOKS FOR YOUNG READERS
New York

Text copyright © 2019 by Emily Butler

Jacket art and interior illustrations copyright © 2019
by Jennifer Thermes

All rights reserved. Published in the United States by Crown Books for Young Readers, an
imprint of Random House Children's Books, a division of Penguin Random House LLC, New York.

Crown and the colophon are registered trademarks of Penguin Random House LLC.

Visit us on the Web! rhcbooks.com

Educators and librarians, for a variety of teaching tools, visit us at RHTeachersLibrarians.com

Library of Congress Cataloging-in-Publication Data
Names: Butler, Emily, author. | Thermes, Jennifer, illustrator.
Title: Freya & Zoose / Emily Butler ; illustrations by Jennifer Thermes.
Other titles: Freya and Zoose
Description: First edition. | New York : Crown Books for Young Readers, [2019] | Summary: Freya,
a penguin, and Zoose, a mouse, become friends while stowaways on Salomon August Andree's
1897 hot air balloon expedition to the North Pole.
Identifiers: LCCN 2018006937 (print) | LCCN 2018014488 (ebook) |
ISBN 978-1-5247-1773-5 (ebook) | ISBN 978-1-5247-1771-1 (hardcover) |
ISBN 978-1-5247-1772-8 (glb)
Subjects: | CYAC: Adventure and adventurers—Fiction. | Stowaways—Fiction. | Hot air balloons—
Fiction. | Andrée, Salomon August, 1854–1897—Fiction. | Explorers—Fiction. | Penguins—Fiction.
| Mice—Fiction. | Arctic regions—Fiction.
Classification: LCC PZ7.1.B89327 (ebook) | LCC PZ7.1.B89327 Fre 2019 (print) | DDC
[Fic]—dc23

The text of this book is set in 12-point Century Schoolbook Pro.
Book design by Maria T. Middleton

Printed in the United States of America

10 9 8 7 6 5 4 3 2 1

First Edition

To Sarina, who is held dear
by both Freya *and* Zoose

CHAPTER
One

There was no question in Freya's mind that this was her last chance. Either she would find a way onto the balloon, or she would live out the rest of her days on this miserable rock. The men down on the beach nailed the boards of the balloon house together, a shed with no roof. The wind carried parts of their conversation up to Freya's hideout. From these snippets she knew that she had three nights to prepare for the journey. That was how much time she had to gather the courage to leave.

Men had been here once before, a year ago. They had

built the same shed, filled the balloon with gas, and then watched helplessly as the wind knocked it to the ground. They'd left with their tails between their legs. Freya had lacked the gumption to try her luck with that crew, but another year of solitude had almost driven her mad; now she'd do anything to get off the island. And there was something else: she wasn't a spring chick anymore. If she was going to save herself, it was now or never. *No guts, no glory,* she thought. Hideous expression.

As the sun began to sink toward the edge of the sea, the men rowed themselves back to their big ship, where they ate and laughed and slept. Freya waddled down to the balloon house and slipped inside. Here she saw the great basket, not yet rigged to the balloon, in the middle of the floor. Would there be room for her and her things? The wicker was densely woven, but she gripped a piece in her beak and tugged. After an hour or so of this, she unraveled a gap large enough to squeeze through.

And what luck! Once inside, she realized that the basket was made of not one but two layers of wicker, with cotton stuffed between them for warmth. Freya plucked some of it out and made a small compartment for herself. "Third-class passage," she sniffed, "but it will do."

Then there was much to-ing and fro-ing between the basket and her hideout, as she toted her supplies down to the shed and concealed them in her little berth. She ferried tins of sardines and stale biscuits. There was coffee powder that tasted faintly of dirt, and some mysterious potted meat. Precious packets of Baldwin's Nervous Pills were squirreled away, as was a suitcase crammed with extra sweaters and a lilac-colored woolen scarf.

Exhausted by this effort, Freya wove the wicker back together and hurried to her cave to rest. On the second night, she was at work again. This time she packed some cakes of chocolate, several items of a personal nature, a suet pudding that was probably five years past its prime, and many strips of bitter green moss that was said to prevent scurvy. Then she went home and crouched at the mouth of her cave to watch the activity on the shore.

Men scurried this way and that. Some measured the speed and direction of the wind. Others oiled ropes and checked the contents of wooden chests. Freya saw the glint of brass nautical instruments. And above it all rose the glorious balloon, shining and rippling in the sun, growing more rotund by the hour as the men pumped it full of hydrogen.

Freya stroked her beloved copy of *Hints to Lady Travellers at Home and Abroad* one last time to calm her nerves. How difficult the decision to leave the book behind had been. She could not in good conscience add any weight to the basket that wasn't strictly necessary to her survival— hadn't she snipped the very fringe off her boots to make them lighter? Anyway, she had long since memorized every word written by Mrs. Davidson, the woman who had governed her adventures.

"My *adventure*," Freya corrected herself out loud. There had only been one so far, and look how that had turned out. Misadventure, more like. Tragedy, even!

On the third night, Freya played a last round of checkers for old times' sake. Then she dropped the black and white pebbles out of the cave and listened to them skitter down the side of the cliff. It had taken her months to collect them, but there was nothing more depressing than playing checkers against oneself, even if one was guaranteed to win every time. She had come to despise the pebbles and the lonely way their clinks echoed off the walls of the cave. Good riddance to bad rubble, indeed!

She filled her canteens with water from the spring, and then there was almost nothing left for her to do except sweep out the cave with beach grass, which she did with scrupulous care. Freya removed *Hints to Lady Travellers* from its nook in the cave wall and cradled it in her wing. "I fear I've become strange," she admitted to its faded cover. Her final act was to heap some stones over the book, making a sort of tomb. She stood before the mound for a full minute. Then she buttoned her jacket, picked up her canteens, and made her way to the shed on the seashore.

For the third and last time, Freya breached the basket and squeezed herself into the familiar cavity. She did her best to repair the wicker from the inside and waited for the sun to come up. Her heart drummed in her ears. Was she afraid she might be discovered? Was she anxious to begin the journey? She was many things, but mostly she was determined to leave.

At dawn, she heard the men pull their skiffs up on the gravelly beach. Their jovial voices broke the endless monotony of the surf as their boots pounded the sand, stomping to the shed where the balloon was docked. It billowed up, lofty as a mountain, straining at the ropes that held it to the ground. Freya peered out of the gaps in the wicker basket, which was finally being shackled to the balloon. Oh, the excitement was almost electric! Today was the day, all right.

A tall man, straight as a rod and dressed beautifully in a dark blue jacket, spoke to the small assemblage inside the shed. This was Salomon August Andrée, and he was the captain. His blond mustache shook with authority and dash. Phrases like "we intend to act" and "the weather favors our success" rolled off his tongue and settled over the crowd like a blessing. He lifted his arm to salute the balloon, whose silken panels shimmered back at him obediently.

Next to the captain stood Nils the photographer. For weeks, Freya had watched him carry his black box here and there, making pictures of the expedition. Now his equipment was stored safely inside the basket, but he still observed his companions closely, as if trying to compose their portraits. And Freya knew something the others did not: when nobody was looking, Nils pulled a gold locket from inside his shirt and pressed it to his lips.

The third member of the crew was named Knut, and wasn't he everyone's favorite? He was frisky, reminding Freya of the young reindeer she had known in Sweden, though she doubted any one of them could do the trick Knut did on the beach, walking through the surf on his hands.

Captain Andrée's remarks were interrupted when a man carrying an official-looking clipboard entered the shed and strode through the group with great ceremony. He relayed his information, punctuating it with some taps of a pencil against the clipboard. A squall was blowing in from the south. Perhaps they should wait one more day. The captain's mustache bristled fiercely as he weighed the man's words. "No," he said. "No. We will sail above the clouds. You will see us again in a year—or perhaps two years."

"I beg you to reconsider. The North Pole will still be there if you leave tomorrow, or the next day, or on Friday!" insisted the man with an urgent tap of his pencil.

"On Friday, the North Pole will fly the flag of Sweden!" said Captain Andrée.

This brought many cheers of "Hurrah!" from the men, and the captain led his crew to the balloon. Freya was elated as they climbed aboard. They stood above her, and she couldn't see them through the sailcloth that lined the inside of the basket. But she could hear them, and she listened joyfully as the captain gave instructions as to how the shed should be dismantled, and dictated a message to be telegraphed to the newspaper.

Then it truly was time to go. "Cut the ropes!" commanded

Captain Andrée. This was done, and Freya felt the unnatural sensation of rising off the ground. Her wings weren't engineered to lift her body from the earth, and she accepted that limitation of her species. Most penguins of good breeding felt as she did, that grandiose notions of flying were in poor taste. Still, a part of her had always wondered what it would be like to soar through the air. Now she was about to find out.

Peering through the outer basket, she saw the caps on the men's heads sink beneath her. Then the balloon rose above the walls of the shed, and she could see the cliff and bits of gray sky and some falling snow. The basket swung back and forth as if rocked by an invisible hand. *I'm as safe as a baby in a cradle!* thought Freya, nestling into the cotton wadding of her dim cocoon. *Ah, how lovely. Flying is really the only way to travel!*

Her stomach lurched as the balloon soared higher, but this was eclipsed by a wave of good cheer that swelled into something almost ecstatic as the distance between Freya and the island lengthened. She might just as well have been trapped underneath that pile of stones as on top! They had crushed her a little more each day. At the end, right before the men had come back, she sensed that maybe she had become a stone herself, hardly able to move or feel. But now her nightmare was over. She felt nearly weightless, and she relaxed as the misery of the past year drained away. It was replaced by a warm delirium. Freya eased herself against the cotton, stretching her legs out as far as they could go.

Then something pushed back. "Watch it, lady!" came a squeak from the darkness. "You ain't the only oyster in the stew!"

CHAPTER

⚡ TWO ⚡

Freya's rapture shriveled up like a raisin. "Kindly iden-
tify yourself!" she demanded, rattled and angry at the
assault on her brief happiness.

"All right, all right," the voice answered. "No need to get
your feathers in a bunch. The name's Zoose."

"What are you doing in my cabin?" asked Freya. She
twisted around and looked behind her, trying to make out
the intruder.

"Your cabin? You've got to be joking. I've been living in
this basket ever since they built it."

Gradually the voice acquired a shape, and Freya was

able to see a furry little face with a pointy nose and two eyes that glittered brazenly. Zoose was a mouse. Freya was neutral on the subject of mice, having never had much to do with them. But she doubted that they made desirable traveling companions. One did not hear tales of illustrious mice on grand adventures. And this one, small and shifty as he was, looked like a rogue.

"You should have made your presence known to me at once," she said.

"Oh, yeah? Why's that?" asked the mouse. "Is it a rule?"

"No," said Freya. "It's just polite."

The balloon took a sudden plunge through the air, and both voyagers clung to the basket walls instinctively, Freya with her beak and Zoose with his paws. They listened to the commotion above them. Captain Andrée shouted to Nils and Knut to toss various things overboard, and as they carried out his orders, the basket swung and bobbed fiercely.

"What's going on?" Freya asked. "Why are we bouncing around like this?"

"Haven't the foggiest idea," said the mouse.

"But you said you've lived in here from the beginning."

"And so I have. But this is the first time the basket's ever been aloft. I don't know any more about aeronautics than your average earthworm. Or penguin."

The nerve of him! thought Freya. Was he insulting her intelligence? Or insinuating that she was average? The balloon steadied itself and resumed its progress through the sky. She looked once again through the wicker and tried to enjoy the crisp outline of the island as it receded into the distance. The water was etched with whitecaps that formed regular and reassuring patterns. But Freya was unsettled. She decided to take control of the situation by introducing herself.

"My name is Freya," she said, sounding more imperious than she had intended. "I'm from Sweden. This is my second voyage, so I am not entirely without travel experience."

"I've lost count of my 'voyages,'" stated Zoose with something like a smirk. "Ran out of fingers and toes."

Freya ignored this possible challenge. "Where do you come from?" she asked. It was courteous to adopt an attitude of interest.

"London," he said.

"You're a long way from home, aren't you?" she said.

"Not really," said Zoose.

Contradicting people seemed to come very easily to this mouse, a quality Freya found most disagreeable. She resolved not to ask him any more personal questions, but Zoose continued speaking. "Home is wherever I kick off my boots. I haven't seen the family in years."

"How they must miss you," said Freya drily.

"Doubt it. My mother had a hundred and eighty-one children by the time I came along. We slept in a sock and had to take turns."

Was there any way to terminate this conversation? "That sounds dreadful," said Freya.

"On the contrary. Ma did the best she could. Gave me a kiss and pushed me out the door when I was two years

old—best thing that could have happened to me. Anyway, who needs family? If you've seen one mouse, you've seen them all."

Freya's attempt to mask her horrified expression made him laugh. "I'm joking, of course! Mice are as different as snowflakes. Except for the babies—our own mothers can't tell us apart. We all look like miniature sausages. You could stick toothpicks in us and serve us as appetizers. Nobody would know the difference."

This was beyond appalling. Freya began to contemplate her luck. Where traveling was concerned, she seemed to have very little. It was entirely possible that she was stuck with this mouse for the rest of the voyage, unless he accidentally dropped through a hole in the bottom of the basket, which was unlikely. Not that she wished him any harm, but to find oneself in close quarters with someone so vulgar was hard. All things being equal, it struck her as grossly unfair.

"May I ask you," she said, "how you came to join this expedition?"

"What do you mean?" asked the mouse.

"I mean that we may be penned in here for some time. It would put our minds at ease if we communicated our intentions. I'd like to know what you're doing in a balloon that is sailing for the North Pole," said Freya. "Oh, and what your plans are, once we get there."

Zoose leaned toward Freya, who retreated an inch or two. "Not much to tell. I spent a few years bumming around Europe until I wound up in Sweden, which was the end of the line, more or less. I said to myself, 'This is decent enough. Why don't I settle down right here?' And I found me an empty room behind a cabinet in a woodworker's shop in Stockholm. Do you know Henriksson's, down on Kåkbrinken Street? Well, one day a fellow with a fine mustache comes in, the one flying this balloon—"

"Captain Andrée," inserted Freya.

"The captain," agreed Zoose. "And he starts talking to Henriksson, who runs the shop, describing a contraption he wants built to hang underneath a balloon that will carry him all the way to the North Pole. Says he's going to be the first person to get there, and that a balloon is the best way to go. Says it's never been done before, but it's perfectly safe with the air currents being what they are. He's got it all plotted. I'm listening to the whole conversation, thinking there's no way I'm going to miss out on this one. So Henriksson builds the basket, and I make sure there's a place for me, see? When the captain has it shipped to the island, I'm already aboard, snug as a bug in a rug."

"But what will you do when we land?" Freya asked.

"It's not what I'll *do;* it's what I'll *be*. And that's the first mouse to explore the North Pole," Zoose said. "I never worry about what I'll do. Doing is what happens along the way."

Freya found her companion's lack of planning unimpressive, but before she could say another word, the balloon gave a tremendous lurch. Then it began to plummet. Uneasy, she braced herself against the woven walls with outstretched wings.

"This is not the smooth sailing one might hope for," she said.

"It never is," said Zoose placidly.

Once again there was much commotion in the basket above their berth as the men raced around, trying to coax the balloon to fly higher. Zoose pressed a large round ear to the inner basket and listened for a moment. Then he nod-ded knowingly.

"For heaven's sake, what's going on?" Freya asked.

"We're having a problem with the sun, on account of its being too hot," said Zoose. "The man with the camera has it all figured out."

"You mean Nils," she said.

"That's the one. He reckons that when the balloon rises, the sun warms the gas inside and it takes up more space. You know how that business works, right?"

"Yes, of course, gas expands when heated," said Freya. "I did go to school, once upon a time."

"Not me," said Zoose. "But I'm a fast learner. So the gas gets bigger and spills out of the balloon. Then she sinks. This old girl has eight million holes pricked in her, in case that's news to you. They're mostly covered with varnish. Mostly."

Freya felt the first tingling of panic and squelched it firmly. "Holes, you say? I wasn't aware of any holes."

"Millions of 'em," repeated Zoose. "The captain told Henriksson that the balloon was sewn together by a dozen lovely ladies in Paris who put in eight million stitches. And every time their needles stabbed through the silk, what did they make? A teeny, tiny hole. And what might seep out of that hole and make its escape? A little molecule of hydrogen, the very thing that's supposed to keep us up in the air!"

Freya was impressed by the mouse's understanding of molecular science, a subject she found rather perplexing. But she sensed that he was playing on her nerves.

"This knowledge did not deter you from making the voyage, I see," she said.

"Not for a minute. Like I said, the holes are mostly covered with a varnish invented by the captain himself. Top-secret stuff, boiled eel skin and tree sap and whatnot. But Nils thinks some of the holes might be releasing gas anyway, the closer we get to the sun."

"Then the problem corrects itself!" said Freya. "The balloon lets out some gas, moves away from the sun, and all is well."

"Ah," said Zoose, "but what if she sinks too far and we wind up in the ocean?"

He was plainly enjoying her discomfort, and she resolved to keep her qualms to herself. After all, traveling entailed risks, and one had to rise to the occasion. And rise she would, just like the balloon.

Unfortunately, the balloon wasn't rising. It was sinking, and not in the manner of a bird making a graceful descent. No, it was more like a cheap yo-yo on a knotted string. It dropped and then stopped suddenly, snagged on a current

of air that might send it back up or just tumble it about a bit. Then it would drop again, spastically, before zigging left or right. Finally, the balloon gave up altogether and plummeted toward the water, where the basket landed with a wet slap.

Not good, not good, worried Freya, whose berth was now just inches above sea level. She could feel the damp coming up from the bottom of the basket. Freya had no fear of water, though it had been years since she'd swum recreationally. From her perspective, there was nothing

especially terrifying about being lobbed into the ocean. But she was a penguin, not a fish. She wouldn't last long if she was trapped in a wicker basket under the water. "Perish the thought!" she said out loud. Then, sheepish, she glowered at Zoose in case he was inclined to mock her. The mouse said nothing at all, but watched and listened with ears pricked and nose quivering.

As the balloon struggled to rise, things only got worse. The basket jolted and jounced over the surface of the ocean, and Freya was tossed around like a rag doll. If she hadn't packed herself in so tightly, she might have been seriously injured. As it was, Zoose was thrown against her quite violently.

"Oh, do be careful!" she implored as he smacked into her shoulder.

"I've had taxi rides worse than this!" yelled Zoose as he somersaulted backward into the dark, referring in gasps to "every pothole in London." Then he was buried in some cotton stuffing and temporarily silenced.

Freya listened to the men inside the basket. "The sand, Knut, the sand! Dump it all, every last bag!"

"But, Captain!" Knut exclaimed. "That's five hundred and fifty pounds of ballast! What if we need it when we reach north?"

"The only thing we'll need is life jackets if we don't get off the water! Lose the sand!" bade Captain Andrée. There was a note in his voice that Freya hadn't heard before. She was sure he would offer almost anything to the sea if it would only let go of the basket.

Plish! Plosh! Bag after bag of sand was thrown overboard, and bit by bit the sea loosened its grip. The crew cheered as the balloon, lighter now by a quarter ton, lifted itself into the air. Freya heard them clap each other on the back, elated to be flying again. The cause for alarm had passed! She herself felt almost giddy, an emotion more foreign to her than any other. With more space, she might have danced a little jig.

"There we are, right as rain again!" she said to Zoose, who was picking cotton out of his whiskers. He looked pale behind his fur. Freya was so full of relief that some of it flowed over into concern for the mouse. "Buck up, now. We're back on track!"

"I wish we were on track—a railroad track, that is. Trains are how I like to travel," admitted Zoose. "I don't relish being this far off the ground."

"Well, *I* do," said Freya. Now that they were newly airborne, she was savoring the idea of her own birdliness more than she could possibly have imagined. Of course, she was every bit the land dweller that the mouse was. Yet she did have feathers. "*I* feel like I'm in my element!" she exulted.

Then the basket heaved again, buffeted by the wind, and Freya smacked her head against her suitcase.

"How's your element now?" muttered Zoose, who was upside down and missing a shoe.

"Oh, shut up," she whimpered as the basket creaked and shuddered. Things only grew more difficult as the sky darkened. The balloon was battered by gusts of cold wind that did not let up for a minute, and Freya was amazed when Zoose burrowed deep into the cotton and began to snore.

There was no sleep for her that night, not a wink.

CHAPTER

~ Three ~

As pinpoints of light filtered into the basket, Freya hoped her frightful ordeal was over. She was proud of herself. Her resolve had been tested and had not been found lacking. She was frazzled in body, but her mind was vigorous! The abominable motions of the basket were waning—now it seemed unhurried and purposeful. And she'd been through far worse, Freya told herself. Today would be a piece of cake.

Cake! Truth be told, Freya wasn't hungry in the least. Her stomach was rumbly, as if she'd swallowed a pailful of pollywogs. But Mrs. Davidson was very specific on the point of breakfast: *After a long night journey, breakfast is an absolutely necessary consideration, and a really good meal should be taken.* Freya lacked the makings of a really good meal, but she did have a tin of sardines she'd been saving. Under normal circumstances, it would be rude to open such a smelly item in a small space shared with other travelers. But the mouse was still asleep, and Freya suspected he was used to any number of strong odors. She stuck her beak into one of her food parcels and extracted a tin can.

"Oooh, something smells scrummy!" said Zoose, poking his nose out of his burrow and catching Freya in the very act of taking her first bite. "Nothing like waking up to a whiff of sardines. Hits you like a punch in the face, and I mean that in a very good way."

The appetizing crunch of tiny bones held no appeal in the presence of this irritating stranger, who emerged from his nest, nose all aquiver. So much for breakfast. *Travel is the true touchstone of character,* Mrs. Davidson admonished. Well, she would not be selfish. She extended the tin in his direction. "Help yourself," she said.

"Don't mind if I do," said Zoose, seizing the food with delight. He nibbled the flesh off each fish as neatly as corn off the cob, pulling the spiny remains from his mouth and smacking his lips with gusto. Freya felt her stomach heave, and she pressed her face to the basket, reviving herself with deep, cold breaths.

A little civility goes a long way in traveling, she remembered. "Did you sleep well?" she asked, ignoring the gulping and offensive sighs of pleasure coming from the mouse.

"Like a log," said Zoose between oily mouthfuls. "It was

like being back in the sock with my brothers, but even better. I feel sorry for anyone that's never been rocked to sleep by a balloon!"

"Rocked to sleep, were you? I'm astonished. The balloon was whacked about like a tennis ball all night long. We rode through a storm, you know," said Freya.

"Didn't feel it," said Zoose, handing back the empty tin. "I'm fresh as a daisy. You should eat something—food will set you straight!"

"You don't say," grumbled Freya. She put the tin away. "I could probably manage a plain breakfast bun, if I had one. Which I do not."

"But I do! I happen to have a plain breakfast bun—well, part of one, at least. We'll just brush off the dirt where it got stepped on, and presto! Good as new!" said Zoose. But no sooner had he turned to rummage through his things than the basket slammed into something solid, pitching the mouse backward and into the softest part of Freya's belly. She felt the air whoosh out of her. Then *bump!* went the basket, and Freya whirled around, slipped and fell on top of Zoose, who struggled in vain to free himself from her superior bulk. This back-and-forth went on for several minutes until, during a momentary lull, Freya managed to peek through the basket.

"Oh, no! We're on the ice!" she cried. "We've come down
too far. We're flying too low!"

Zoose angled himself against the side of the basket and
took a look. It was true. The basket scraped along a field of
ice that extended as far as the eye could see. It crashed into
every jagged ridge and wrinkle in its path. As solidly built
as it was, nevertheless it would be smashed to bits if the
balloon didn't gain some altitude.

"We've left the water behind us, at least," said Zoose. "Maybe this is the North Pole? Not much to look at, is it?"

But the rate at which the humans were casting out ballast told Freya that they had not arrived at the North Pole. There was a frenzy of activity above her, and through her peephole she saw a massive anchor fall over the side of the basket and land with a heavy thud.

"Not the instruments!" she heard the captain shout. "Remember our duty to science!"

There was some discussion, and the anchor was followed by a really splendid medicine chest. Then a large wooden buoy was jettisoned; a familiar blue-and-yellow flag popped from its top and fluttered handsomely on the way down.

"God save the king," said Freya. Surely the captain had meant to claim the glory of discovering the North Pole for Sweden with that flag. Well, it wasn't important.

"Ah, now, that's a shame," lamented Zoose as several crates marked with the words *Champagne* were cast overboard. These sacrifices bought a few feet of lift, but not nearly enough to allow the balloon to clear the formations that jutted high above the ground and menaced the balloon and its cargo.

The adventurers drifted at the mercy of the wind, which

sometimes bashed them into the ice and sometimes left them suspended and going nowhere at all. They had no way to steer the craft and nothing left to dump, at least nothing that wasn't vital to their success once they landed. Sleep was out of the question: the moment one closed one's eyes with fatigue, the balloon plunged downward and collided with the ground, where it was pulled for yards like a prisoner being dragged from his cell to the gallows.

And so it went on, unrelentingly. "A novel form of punishment, this is," Freya quipped weakly. "We must have done something awful in a past life to deserve it. And I don't even believe in past lives."

The mouse made no response to her feeble joke. She peered at him closely and thought he looked a little green about the whiskers. He held his head in his paws and periodically clutched his stomach. She felt positively seasick herself, and by the sounds of it, so did the humans.

By the time the meager Arctic sun began to set, Freya

had resorted to her trick of chanting multiplication tables. The alternative was to lose one's mind, although it possibly amounted to the same thing.

When she had gone all the way through the thirteens twice, she turned to poems, which she recited aloud. Her favorite one began like this:

It is an ancient Librarian
Who stops to talk with me.
Her bearded chin and milky eyes
Are things I can't unsee!

She holds me with her withered hand.
"There was a book," croaks she.
"Back off! Don't touch me, crazy bat,
Or I shall count to three!"

"Count away, thou dunderhead,"
Hisses the Librarian.
"But hear the tale, for soon you'll be
A moldering mound of carrion. . . ."

"Carrion?" asked Zoose.

"It means 'dead and rotting flesh,'" explained Freya.

"I knew it!" groaned the mouse, pausing until a wave of nausea passed. "You might as well ask Death to ride with us in this balloon!"

"Fiddlesticks. It's just a poem," said Freya.

"It's an invitation," insisted Zoose.

"What superstitious nonsense. Every schoolchild in Sweden knows this poem by heart. It's as famous as—"

She was interrupted by an atrocious bash as the basket scudded into another hummock of solid ice.

"No more poems about death," said Zoose as they swung furiously from side to side.

"As a matter of fact, it's a poem about a book," said Freya. (*And also about death,* she admitted to herself.)

There was no more conversation in the darkening basket, and the voyagers spent another night trying to ignore how unbearably tired they were becoming. The balloon doddered along now, unable to hurdle the lowest ridges and hitting everything in its path. Not even the mouse could rest. By the dawning of the third day, it was clear that something would have to be done.

"We can't go on like this," said Zoose. "They need to bring down the balloon."

"Aren't you worried?" asked Freya.

"Not a bit," said Zoose. "It's just a matter of finding a straight spit of ice and letting out some hydrogen, nice and slow. We'll come down like a feather on a mattress. You'll see."

"Well, I expect Captain Andrée is the man to do it. After all, he's flown balloons before."

Zoose snorted. "*I* could do it, and the only thing I've ever flown is a kite, when I was no bigger than a bottle cap. Nothing to it—you just pull on a string."

Freya was certain it was more complicated than that, but she lacked the energy to argue. She wasn't sure she could say one more word. She had never been this exhausted in her life. What if she started to hear voices, or to see things that weren't there? Nothing was distinct inside their dim cabin, but even so, shapes were beginning to weave and wobble in a very strange way. The mouse, for example, resembled a very large pincushion once belonging to her late aunt Agatha. She looked away.

The end was quick and merciful. Hammered by the elements during its flight, the balloon was now coddled in its final descent, tenderly caressed by the wind as it sank onto the ice. Freya felt a slight bump as the basket touched down. Then it slowly tipped over and came to rest on its side.

"That's it?" she asked, unprepared for this mellow conclusion to such a grueling, sleepless passage. *Could it all be over?*

"What, did you think we was going to burst into flames or something?" chuckled Zoose as he vanished from the basket.

Where the mouse went was of no concern to Freya, nor did she hear his parting words. The most she could manage to do was pull her padded jacket around herself and curl up into a ball. *Is any of this real?* she wondered. *Have I flown across the ocean? Is this what I chose?* She was engulfed by sleep before she could think of any answers.

When Freya awoke, the absurdity of her predicament dawned on her. She was lodged with her few possessions inside a basket, in unfamiliar territory, with no means of transportation, and her peculiar companion was gone. In other words, she was in a real pickle. One might almost despair.

Freya unraveled the wicker until she opened a hole through which she might leave the basket, and emerged onto a vast frozen plain. White light drove itself like darts into her eyes. She cringed, blinking rapidly until she became accustomed to the harsh glare of sun on snow. Then she stumbled forward, her legs stiff and uncooperative after the cramped confinement of the voyage. When she had put some distance between herself and the basket, she turned around and took stock of the situation. There was the balloon, stretched flat on the ground, a dark stain on the ice. It was well and truly dead.

On the other side of the gulf of deflated silk panels stood Nils, who was taking pictures of the captain and young Knut as they set up camp. *That man's a true optimist,* thought Freya. Then she gazed at the endless landscape behind the men, its breadth scarred by sharply crested peaks. In some places the snow was mottled with pools of rotten ice. "Terra incognita," she murmured.

"Terra what?" asked Zoose, who had been standing next to her for who knew how long.

"It means 'unknown land,'" said Freya. "At least, unknown to me. Maybe if I had an atlas, I could establish what country—"

"No, you couldn't," said Zoose before she'd even finished.

"What do you mean, I couldn't? I'll have you know I'm very handy with an atlas." This mouse would insist on contradicting her to the bitter end.

"You couldn't because we're not on land, known or unknown. We're on an ice floe, or so the captain says," explained Zoose. "We're on a mass of ice, and we're floating around the ocean, probably crashing into other masses of ice."

"That's ridiculous," said Freya. "Look about yourself—the ground goes on for miles and miles. Ice floe, indeed!"

"Oh, it's a big one, all right. I hiked for ages and didn't get anywhere near the edge of it," said Zoose. "Thought I'd strike out on my own, but now I'm not so sure."

"You're staying with the humans, then?" asked Freya.

"Yeah, and you will too, if you know what's good for you. After all, they brought compasses and maps." They looked at Captain Andrée, who was at this very moment spreading maps onto a makeshift table and unpacking something he called his sextant. "They also brought cheese. 'When in doubt, the cheese wins out,' right? That's just common sense."

Four

The penguin and the mouse decided to stay in the basket while Captain Andrée and his crew camped. This was for the sake of convenience, more than anything. The basket was warm and snug—a bit too snug, in Freya's opinion, and she made another space for herself a little farther away from the mouse's berth. She found his habit of slyly breaking off a piece of wicker and picking his teeth with it almost unbearable. *Real annoyance from fellow travelers should never be endured,* Mrs. Davidson had counseled. Well, this probably didn't rise to the level of "real annoyance," like blowing one's nose without a hand-kerchief, but it came very close.

"Freya," he said, pulling a splinter out of his mouth. "Freya. That's an uncommon name. I guess your ma made it up?"

"Certainly not!" she corrected him. "My parents named me after the goddess Freya, who governs love, beauty, death, and . . ." She faltered, remembering the mouse's sour reaction the last time she'd alluded to the subject of death. In fact, Zoose was looking at her through narrowed eyes this very minute. "Or rather," Freya continued, "she rules over the place where half the warriors who die in combat go after they're"—Zoose grimaced—"killed." Zoose made a disparaging sound in his throat and shook his head in disgust. "Only half of them, mind you!" Freya hastened to add. Then she stopped talking.

After a long and unsettling pause, Zoose spoke again. "So, have you seen this goddess Freya? Spoken to her?"

She looked at him curiously. "Of course I haven't. She's just a myth—she's in our stories. She wears a cloak of feathers, which I suspect is really why my parents chose the name. Our priest didn't care for it, but then again, he wasn't consulted."

"Oh? Did he curse you?"

Freya thought about Father Josef, a portly penguin who often showed up just as the family was sitting down to supper and always obliged them by accepting the biggest dish of rice pudding. "No," she said. "He didn't go in for cursing, much."

"I'm named after a god as well—Zeus, the god of all gods," said Zoose importantly.

"Is that a family name?" asked Freya, to be polite.

"Not that I know. My mother went through the alphabet to come up with names. Every time she came to a twenty-sixth child, she had to think of something starting with Z. Zach and Zero were already taken. So was Zane, Zealot, Zilch, and Zarathustra. I got Zoose, which I like on account of its having two o's, which is good luck."

"But Zeus doesn't have two o's," objected Freya. "And why would that be good luck, even if it did?"

"You don't know much about luck, do you?" said Zoose. "Or spelling. Anyway, it's not bad being named after the top dog, I guess, although he's never done anything for me. I don't really like religion, as such."

"For goodness' sake, why not?" asked Freya.

"To begin with, I was never allowed to worship the bones of our ancestors, like everyone else. The priest wouldn't let me near them. So before I left, I stole them all and dropped them in the river. I suppose that's why things go wrong for me—my ancestors are still mad about it."

Freya didn't know what to say. She gaped at Zoose with her beak hanging open.

"What?" he asked. "I was young. We all make mistakes."

Freya decided it was a good time to take some air. She

clambered out of the basket and peeked around the edge
at the humans, who were prying lids off crates and laying
objects on the ground.

Industrious as ants, she thought as Knut grappled with
a long contraption made of dark mahogany. He tugged and
pulled at it, and then called Nils over to help. Freya watched
in fascination as the thing expanded smoothly into a frame-
work composed of a wooden spine and gracefully curved ribs.
It was evident to her that the men were not building something so much as unfolding it, but what it was she couldn't
say. Were they setting up a sort of skeleton wigwam for shelter? That was prudent of them, but then what to make of the
excellent tent that Captain Andrée was erecting nearby? As
the minutes passed, Freya's curiosity grew until she was in
an absolute fervor. What in creation were they doing, and
why? Nils and Knut laid some planks across the open part
of the thingamabob, bolting them deftly to its sides. Then
Freya felt like a nitwit for not having seen it straightaway.

"They're building a boat," she told the mouse breath-
lessly, imparting this information through the hole in the
basket. "Come and see it! Flying to the North Pole didn't
work, but rowing there might."

Zoose left the basket and followed Freya. Sure enough, a
fine boat had taken shape.

"They'll never get to the North Pole in that thing," said Zoose as Nils and Knut finished covering the vessel with a canvas skin.

"Why ever not?" asked Freya.

"It's too small. It won't carry three humans and their baggage—not even close. I reckon they'll drag it to the edge of one ice floe and ferry themselves over to the next. Then they'll row back and forth until they've brought all their things across, and do it again."

Freya imagined what a lot of work that would be.

"And are you thinking what I'm thinking?" continued Zoose.

"I very seriously doubt it," said Freya.

"That boat's our next ride," announced Zoose.

"What are you driving at?" asked Freya. "I'm sure if they catch us inside, we'll be invited to leave, and none too nicely."

"Then they better not catch us," said Zoose.

Freya didn't like to think of herself as sneaky, and the idea of stowing away on the boat seemed altogether too underhanded. "I'm not sure that's very sporting, if you know what I mean. Is it fair for us to add to their load? The humans are doing all the work, and we contribute nothing."

Zoose snorted. "What did you contribute to our balloon ride?"

"That was a unique proposition," replied Freya. "In the case of the balloon ride, the balloon did all the work. Or at least almost all of it. I was not an impediment to the men. They did no extra labor on my account!"

Zoose shrugged, unmoved by the logic of her argument.

"I did not contribute to the venture, but neither did I abuse anyone's hospitality," Freya said.

"I'm not planning to abuse anyone, if that's what you're getting at," said Zoose. "The boat won't know we're stowed away any more than the balloon did."

"Now you're being dense," said Freya. "The men will have to move the boat, and us along with it. What will we do for them in return?"

"Not a thing," said Zoose, "and trust me, we'll all be the better for it. As far as I can tell, you flimflammed your way onto the balloon, same as me. This is no different."

"I did no such thing," huffed Freya. "And in any case, I was in dire straits."

"You still are," he said.

Freya walked away with all the dignity she could muster. She refused to explain herself to a creature who had been raised in a sock. It was possibly not even his fault that he was so unpleasant, but a penguin could only take so much.

As she picked her way across the ice, she studied her situation. She had cast her lot in with the humans from the moment she poked her beak into their basket. Of course she had. The only way she was getting off this floating lump of ice was by sticking to them like damp newspaper. All the same, one wanted to be decent about it. What had Mrs. Davidson said about a certain species of traveler? *It is really extraordinary to see the way in which people, well bred in all the other affairs of life, will disregard each other's comfort and consult no one's wishes but their own!* Freya knew she was not that sort of penguin. She would not ignore the humans' welfare so that she might ride in ease. She would have to give this some thought.

Freya looked around. From the air, the ice had seemed smooth and easy. It was very much the opposite on the ground. Sharp crystals poked up through a thin layer of crusty snow, and the floe was crisscrossed by ribbons of running water. There were hills and valleys such as one might find on land, only these were brutally hard. And there were outcroppings of ice, rising high into the air and often of an enormous size. The one in front of her looked like a beached whale and was just as impassable. Oh, yes, she'd better stick with Captain Andrée, Nils and Knut. And the mouse.

Waddling back to the basket, Freya watched the humans as they continued to work. Zoose observed them as well, narrating their progress with a stream of commentary that Freya chose to ignore. "Oh, now that looks tasty," he said as Knut stirred a pot balanced on the camp stove. "I could use a bit of that." Knut tipped something that smelled deliciously beefy into the pot. He was evidently the company's cook.

Six or seven yards away, the captain mounted wooden slats on top of long, curved runners. He was utterly absorbed in this task, fitting the planks together like pieces of a puzzle before screwing them down and binding them with rope. By slow degrees a sledge took form. When it was complete, the captain stood on top of the flat bed and jumped up and down a few times. It bore his weight well. The captain broke into a decorous tap dance before leaping to the ground and bowing to Knut and Nils, who clapped their hands with enthusiasm.

"Very high spirits, all things considered," marveled Freya.

"Why shouldn't they be chipper?" asked Zoose. "Just look at them! They have everything under control!"

It was true: the humans were remarkably cheerful as they went about the business of being stranded on the ice. It was as if their plan all along had been to crash the balloon hundreds of miles short of the North Pole, and then set up a camp for the manufacturing of sledges and boats. *What's next?* thought Freya. *A bicycle?* She had to admire their mettle.

Over the next few days, more sledges materialized until there was one for every human. Nils spent his time examining each item that might be useful in an expedition across the ice. He weighed shovels, hooks, boxes of food, his own camera, film, compasses, sailcloth and guns. He even collapsed the silk tent they slept in and weighed that. Careful notes were made in a small book he kept in his pocket. Every ounce was tabulated.

Then he began to divide everything into three piles. The captain and Knut made suggestions, and Nils added and subtracted various objects. When at last he was satisfied, the humans loaded the sledges, strapping the supplies down with oily ropes. Zoose sniffed in the direction of the boat, which was itself tied onto a sledge and filled with essentials.

"There's my carriage," he said. "I'm settling in tonight, because tomorrow it's bon voyage!"

"You're mistaken, I'm sure. They won't abandon so much equipment!" said Freya. Although each sledge was loaded to the gills, the humans were leaving far more than they were taking.

"You could stay here and look after it for them," said Zoose wickedly. "Lonely life, but you're used to that, I guess."

"What a disagreeable thing to say," remarked Freya. "And what a disagreeable mouse you are. Why don't *you* stay with the camp? They'll probably leave a sock or two behind for you to live in."

"Not a chance," said Zoose. "I'll be the first mouse to set paw on the North Pole, or I'll freeze my tail off trying."

"Yes, and a real loss to the world of Arctic exploration that would be," snapped Freya. She was being petty, which (she felt) was unbecoming. She was also greatly at odds with herself. Freya retreated to the basket before Zoose sensed her lack of moral fiber. There she spent the rest of the day evaluating her options. Was there any other way to travel without adding to the fearful weight of the men's sledges? Nothing occurred to her. The mouse was right. They would have to stow away again, like vagabonds. Like tramps.

That night, it was Freya who roused Zoose after the humans had retired to their tent. Together, they secured their belongings and left the basket for the final time. Moving quietly, they slid under the tarpaulin that covered the provisions stored in the boat, shifting parcels to the left and right until they had a little space for themselves. Bunking together seemed unavoidable, but Freya formed a small bulwark of her things and made sure that Zoose was on the other side of it. They pulled a canvas sack marked *Lemon Juice Lozenges* over themselves. It was pitch-black, which did not bother Freya as much as the waiting. Zoose was soon fast asleep, and she forced herself to close her eyes.

They awoke to the familiar sounds of the humans breakfasting on hot tea and sandwiches. Freya herself nibbled at a hard cracker, while Zoose sucked on something that smelled suspiciously lemony. In the lightless interior of the boat, they listened as Captain Andrée honored the balloon, commending it to the snow and ice forever. Then the humans decamped once and for all, packing their tent and kerosene stove and picking up the ropes with which they would drag the hulking sledges. With the first lurch forward, Zoose whispered, "Off and running! It's gangbusters from here on out!"

Only it wasn't gangbusters. Herky-jerky was more like it. Freya felt the sledge move, and stop. Then it moved again, and paused. After a third attempt to gain traction, the sledge came to a complete halt.

"Captain!" came Knut's voice. "One or two friendly nudges from you might give me some momentum!"

Freya heard a pair of boots crunch across the ice in their direction. Then, with a grunt and some good-natured cursing, Knut's sledge lunged ahead. One more powerful shove from Captain Andrée, and they began to advance fitfully toward the North Pole.

"What a beast of burden am I!" laughed Knut.

"A beast of burden!" echoed Zoose with a giggle.

Even Freya had to smile at Knut's turn of phrase. If young Knut knew that his burden contained actual passengers, he might not be so jolly! But it did please her to join in his mirth. They'd faced real peril on this trip and had come through it bravely. Now it looked like the worst was behind them.

"He's as strong as a bull, is our boy Knut!" continued Zoose. "I'll bet my left whiskers he'll lead the pack!"

"Or die trying," added Freya, taking an optimistic bite of her cracker.

Zoose inhaled sharply. "You did *not* just say that," he whispered.

Then the sledge hit a slippery ridge of ice, tipped on its side and slid into a deep pool of meltwater. In the hullabaloo that followed, Freya barely heard Zoose's cry of dismay turn into a gurgle as the water rushed into the boat and over their heads.

ᦔ Five ᦕ

On the ground, it was fair to say that Freya cut a less than impressive figure. But in the water, she was superb. It took two seconds for her mind to clear. She wriggled from under the tarpaulin and kicked herself free of the boat, gliding several yards like an elegant torpedo before turning to survey the disaster.

There were Knut's legs, thrashing about—he must have fallen in with his sledge. The captain and Nils would have to fish him out, thought Freya. That part was easy enough, but what a whopping great bother for everyone! Boxes and bundles came loose and bobbed to the surface of the pool. It would all have to be recovered and dried off. An entire day of labor would be lost, at least! And that pesky mouse would probably catch his death of a . . . Where was he? Where the deuce was Zoose?

Freya swam this way and that, looking for the mouse. Perhaps he had already hoisted himself onto the ice. It was possible that he was trapped inside the boat. How long could a mouse hold his breath? Freya supposed not very long at all. Then she spotted him, a small dark shape clinging to a twist of rope that dangled from the upended sledge. Freya sped to his side, leaving a stream of bubbles behind her.

She surfaced quietly, willing the humans to look the other way. Then again, they were making such a ruckus salvaging their baggage that they were scarcely in a position to notice a bird talking to a mouse. "Swim!" she hissed to Zoose. "Get out of the water before they see us!"

Zoose said nothing, but shook uncontrollably with cold.

"I mean it!" said Freya. "Let go of that rope and start swimming."

"C-c-can't," said Zoose.

"Can't what? Swim, I tell you!" she commanded.

To this, Zoose screwed up his face and clung more tightly to the rope, as buoyant as a lead fishing sinker, or maybe even less. In a flash, Freya understood the situation: the mouse couldn't swim. In addition, he was freezing to death, panting in shallow *hah-hah-hah*s, teeth chattering like dice. Oh, what was it that Mrs. Davidson had advised in the hour of peril? Freya had read the words a thousand times. They came back to her now: *courage and calmness.*

"Courage and calmness," she whispered, and pried Zoose's fingers off the rope with her beak. "Courage and calmness," she repeated, and wedged the mouse under one wing. Propelling herself through the frigid waters in great, lopsided strokes, she reached the edge of the pool at full tilt. Then she dragged him up onto the ice and behind a hummock where they would not be seen. "Courage and calmness," she avowed, thumping his chest with all her might until he coughed up a lungful of water.

From there, Freya worked like one possessed. She stripped off Zoose's shoes and socks and rubbed his frozen feet as energetically as she could between her wings until she was sure his circulation was restored. Then she did the same with his paws. She slapped his cheeks and buffeted his head many times so that the blood would return to his face and brain. "It would raise my temperature, if he

pummeled me!" she told herself, and kept at it until he
began a pathetic mewling.

Peering around the hum-
mock, Freya watched the
captain and Nils as they
revived Knut, who was still
shivering like a wet puppy.
(*Or a wet mouse,* Freya
thought, glancing back at Zoose.)
They peeled off his drenched
clothes and wrapped him
in a reindeer hide. Then
Captain Andrée began to
assemble the camp stove. Nils
busied himself setting up the
tent on a flat stretch of ice some
twenty yards from the slushy
pool. There would be no more
traveling today.

It was now or never. Freya hopped to the boat, lying on
its side where the humans had left it, soggy cargo heaped
in piles on the ground. She identified her own bags and
bundles, as well as Zoose's untidy haversack. In several

quick, silent trips, she dragged everything behind the hummock.

Then she unpacked what until now she had called her Article of Faith—a dusty calfskin pouch Freya had assembled long ago on the recommendation of Mrs. Davidson. *It is wise never to travel unprovided with a small flask of brandy and water, a tiny case of plaster (with scissors) and strong smelling salts*, Mrs. Davidson had advised. With blind obedience, Freya had gathered the items into a bag and zipped it shut, never imagining she might someday need them. Neither had she imagined that the newfangled zipper would weld itself together with rust.

"Blast!" She hooted her frustration. "Blast this blasted thing. I knew it was a gimmick! Who would trust something called a zipper?" She yanked at it savagely until it ripped away from the leather. Then she removed a tin flask, wiped it clean with her sleeve and opened the screw top. Pressing it to Zoose's lips, she watched grimly as the fiery liquid sloshed over his chin. Zoose had stopped shivering and was now as motionless as a rock.

"Smelling salts first, you ninny," Freya scolded herself. She uncorked the green glass bottle and held it under Zoose's nostrils, waving it gently to release its fumes. His whiskers twitched ever so slightly, and he

moaned. She seized the flask and poured two or three drops down his throat. Zoose moaned again and began to tremble.

And thus began a long cycle of vigorous massage, alternating with brandy water and smelling salts, until Freya herself was nearly dead with fatigue. Four or five times she held the green bottle to her own nose, just to stay awake and keen. Finally, when Zoose had stopped shaking, she unbuttoned her jacket and tucked him under her wing. Then she fell asleep, just as the low polar sun began to lighten the sky.

Zoose was the first to stir. He yawned, then stretched his legs as far as he could, digging his heels into Freya's ribs. Then he burrowed into her feathers, pulling her wing around him like a quilt, and sighed with contentment.

"Paradise," he murmured sleepily. "Never thought they'd let me in."

Freya opened her eyes. "You're not in paradise," she said. "You're in my armpit."

"Shhhh," said Zoose. "Shhhh . . ." His voice drifted away like a happy cloud, and he began to snore.

Freya wondered what to do. On the one hand, he'd nearly perished yesterday. And although it was true that he'd been a nuisance up until then, she would hardly have rejoiced if he'd frozen to death. Freya marveled at her own capacity to act in a crisis. If only her family could have witnessed her courage and calmness! Why, she had saved this mouse from a watery grave and spent the night resuscitating him.

She was a regular Florence Penguingale.

On the other hand, she was bone-tired and famished. When Zoose turned to nestle against her with a contented little snort, Freya decided her patient's recovery was complete.

"Rise and shine!" she barked, and stood up, leaving a very startled mouse on the ice. He looked at her with some confusion, and then rubbed his eyes and studied the landscape.

"Took a bath, did I?" he asked at last. His troubled gaze

rested on the edge of the sludge water, just visible from where he lay.

"So to speak," said Freya. "You were floating around in there like an ice cube. I spent last night thawing you out!"

"Sure, it's coming back to me in bits and pieces. I'm not much of a swimmer—I guess you noticed that." Zoose laughed ruefully.

"Ah, well, you came through it. That's the important thing," she said. Then there was an uncomfortable silence, and Freya realized that if she were waiting for Zoose to thank her, she'd be waiting for a very long time. The mouse was even more deficient in the manners department than he was in the swimming department. Awkward creature! She tried to look indifferent as she riffled through her things for a bite to eat.

"Think I'll go see what the crew is up to," said Zoose, scrambling to his feet. He was quite agile for a mouse who had recently been frozen solid.

"They're still asleep," said Freya, even though he was already out of earshot. She munched on some dried moss and pretended it was bacon while she brooded over her next move. It simply would not do to hole up in the boat again and risk another dunking. She was going to have to hoof it, just like the humans. But that did leave her with the problem of shelter. It was all well and good to spend a night under the stars when the sky was clear, but what about when it snowed? And a stiff winter wind might just be the end of the mouse. Not that that was her problem.

The solution lay several hundred yards behind her. Freya reached into her Article of Faith and extracted the silver pair of scissors. Then she scanned the terrain. It was impossible to commit this landscape to memory, it was so hypnotically repetitive. But the tracks made by the sledges were as plain as paint, and she followed them all the way back to the spot where they had made landfall.

There lay the balloon, like a shroud. *To have placed one's trust in several miles of varnished silk,* thought Freya. *Lunacy!* Well, this was no time for philosophizing. She thrust the tip of the scissors into the balloon, puncturing it ruthlessly. Then she began snipping and didn't stop until she'd cut away a sizable piece of the material.

It was wonderfully light stuff. She rolled it up and dragged it back to the hummock where she and Zoose had spent the night. Then she opened her largest bag and retrieved her sewing kit, blessing Mrs. Davidson yet again for the sage counsel to rove no farther than one's front door without thread and needle.

"What are you doing?" asked Zoose, who had suddenly
reappeared.

"It should be obvious that I'm making myself a tent. Making *us* a tent, if you care to lend a hand," said Freya, trying not to sound exasperated. She unfurled the silk and spread it on the ice.

"Don't bother about me," said the mouse. "I'll be moving on as soon as I work out which way is north."

"I see," replied Freya. "Are you leaving before or after you've had breakfast?"

"After, I think," Zoose said.

His nonchalance was infuriating. "I don't wish to interrogate you, but could you explain why you'd rather head north by yourself instead of heading north with present company?"

"Present company isn't heading north. You're heading east, according to the captain. I just listened to their plans, and lucky I did." When Freya made no comment, he continued. "They've given up on the North Pole. Too far away. They're making for some islands to the east, where there's food and a shot at being rescued."

Freya considered this. "That sounds reasonable," she concluded.

"Well, good luck to you. I didn't sign up for reasonable. I signed up to discover the North Pole, and that's where I'm going."

"Are you insane?" Freya asked. "You'll never make it alone. What about 'staying with the humans if you know what's good for you'? What about their compasses and maps? What about their cheese, if it comes to that?"

"Oh, I have some of their cheese," said Zoose, opening his vest to reveal several large hunks of fragrant cheddar. "I'll be fine on my own."

"Yes, you'll be just dandy. You almost died yesterday, in case you've forgotten," Freya retorted.

"And who do I have to thank for that? You. You and all your talk of Death. You might as well have invited Death into the boat with us and then helped him chuck me into the water!" Zoose picked up pawfuls of snow and threw them over his shoulder, chanting defensive spells and stamping his feet seven times.

Freya stared at him in utter incredulity. "The only person inviting Death here is you, if you think you're going to reach the North Pole by yourself."

Zoose clapped his paws over his ears and stamped his feet again. It was all Freya could do to keep from grabbing his shoulders and shaking him. "Death isn't some trickster who tags along if you say his name. Death happens when it happens, and it happens a lot faster when you act like an imbecile!"

When you hide in the basket of a hot-air balloon and fly over the Arctic Sea? came the unbidden thought to Freya's mind. But she wouldn't allow for that sort of foolishness, not now. "You're staying here if I have to stitch you inside the tent!" she shouted at the obstinate mouse, who was chanting at the top of his lungs. She lunged for him, wrenching his sleeve and trying to disengage his paw from his ear so he might listen to some sense!

And so it was that neither Freya nor Zoose noticed the polar bear until it was nearly upon them. No sooner did they feel themselves enveloped in its dark shadow than it struck.

With one swat of a massive paw, it sent Zoose hurtling through the air like a pebble out of a slingshot. He landed on his back and plowed through the snow until he hit a thick hummock. Freya fared worse: the bear struck again and flung her into a bank of freshwater ice that was as hard as granite. She felt the stab of its claws and the bone-crunching solidity of the ice. Then she heard, saw and felt no more.

CHAPTER
~ Six ~

For three days and nights, Freya lay silent and motionless. She had grievous wounds across her ribs from the bear's attack, and though these had bled profusely, they had not proved fatal. However, the blow to her skull where she'd collided with the ice was catastrophic. Now she was engaged in a battle for her life.

Inside herself, in the deepest part that burns slowly until one draws one's very last breath, she tumbled back and back and back. She fell through time as if each year were a flimsy net, too fragile to hold her. One by one, the years gave way like gossamer webs, until at the very end of everything, she was a chick again. She was Baby Frey, the most cherished and long-awaited jewel in her mother's crown.

"You're my twinkle, my moonbeam!" whispered her mother into her ear.

"Our little treasure, our wunderkind!" added her father, stroking the tip of her tiny beak and laughing when she sneezed. Freya felt the velvety feathers of Mother's plush tummy and sighed with happiness. How fine to be their darling chick once more. She had forgotten the way Father smelled of pipe tobacco and cologne. It was the safest, loveliest smell in the world.

Hour upon hour Mother rocked her in her wings, humming lullabies and feeding her spoonfuls of lingonberry jam and cream. When she put Freya down, it was into a crib that was softer than a cloud, and she covered her with the warmest, silkiest blanket imaginable. There she lay, drifting in and out of sleep, listening to Mother's devoted crooning. What were the words? She could almost hear them.

Hush, little baby, don't make a squeak
Or Papa's gonna smack you for a week.

And if that smacking makes you cry
Papa's gonna eat up all your pie.

And if you're hungry that's too bad
You shouldn't have made your Papa mad.

And if you want to run away
Papa won't try to make you stay.

And if you go, then one, two, three
You're the best little mouse a mousey can be.

Well, *that* was certainly odd. Something about the song struck Freya as rather off the mark, and she began to whimper. But Mother made soothing noises, and Freya floated back into a blissful dream. Being a baby was the best thing in the world. If she had any thoughts at all, they were tender and harmonious.

The light on the other side of Freya's eyelids waxed and waned, just as it had when she was inside the egg (a time she remembered with great pleasure). When it was particularly bright, Mother fed her bits of rich custard. She pressed these to Freya's beak, gently coaxing her to swallow the delicious morsels. Freya had never tasted anything so wonderful in her life.

"Come now, my pet. Eat some more for Mother."

Freya obediently opened her mouth, and as she accepted

another bite of custard, Mother came into focus. What a funny, furry face she had! What long whiskers! What a silly bonnet she wore! How stooped and short . . .

"You're not my mother," said Freya.

"You got that right," said Zoose. "And if this is what it's like being a mother, I can see why mine gave me the boot as soon as I could button my shirt. Haven't slept in three days. I'm as worn out as a broom in a dirt house."

Every bone in Freya's body objected as she tried to sit up. She was sore and stiff, right down to the tips of her feathers, and there was a throbbing pain in her side that made her gasp. "Mother, don't leave me!" she wailed, and clutched at the dream that was receding like the foamy tide. It was no use. Mother was gone. She wanted to cry.

In fact, that's just what she did. Freya wept. She wept for the years of her life gone by in a gray, lonely blur. She wept for the bleak months trapped on an island. She wept for Mother, for Father, for Baby Frey—they were all gone now. She was as weak as a kitten, trapped with an irksome rodent, in the middle of nowhere. She positively sobbed.

"Come on," said Zoose from the ground where he had collapsed. "It's not as bad as all that. I made us a tent, see?"

Freya did see, eventually. When the last hot tear had rolled down her cheek, she found herself looking at the inside of a tent. It was propped up with a white staff of some sort. "Your stitching is very neat," she observed without enthusiasm. "Those seams are perfectly straight. Who would have thought it possible?" Her mortification was complete, and there was no reason to censor anything that crossed her mind.

"Thought it possible?" objected Zoose. "I'll have you know that I apprenticed with a tailor in Seville. He used me like a dog, but I did learn a thing or two!"

"You certainly did." Freya noticed that Zoose was ensconced wrist to ankle in a kind of a snowsuit, heavily lined with some sort of material that made him look twice his size. He posed for her, dapper in an outlandishly inflated way.

She herself was lying inside a sleeping bag, warm as toast. "I see you've made good use of the balloon," said Freya, admiring the workmanship, "but what on earth have you filled it with?"

"Cotton from inside the basket," said Zoose with pride. "Have you forgotten? There's bales of the stuff—it's terrific insulation. Used up almost all your thread, I'm afraid."

"Ah, well." Freya pulled the silk under her chin gingerly. "All for a good cause. You haven't been idle."

"That I haven't," agreed Zoose.

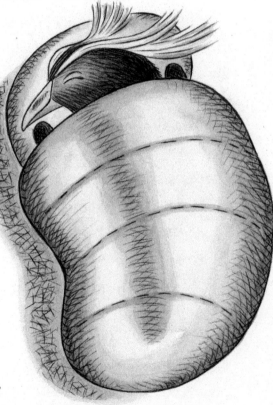

They were quiet for a few minutes, adjusting to the strangeness of this new detente. Freya recalled the overturned boat, and dragging Zoose from the water, and her exertions to keep him alive. She remembered their argument, and then the great, looming bear.

"I thought you were striking out on your own," said Freya. She hesitated to revisit this unpleasantness, but if he was planning to leave, she wanted it out in the open. In any case, if they were to part ways, it was better to do so on friendly terms. "Don't misunderstand me—I'm terribly grateful that you stuck around after the attack."

"Of course I stuck around. I'm not some riffraff who skips out in an emergency. I mean, I'll abandon ship when I have to. That is to say, if it's a choice between me and drowning, I'll save myself. . . ." Zoose broke off, in some confusion. "I mean, I *was* drowning. I know it. I know you saved me. Fair's fair, right? Of course I stuck around."

"Well, it was good of you," said Freya. "And if the bear comes back, why, I'll just have to be on my toes."

Zoose laughed with some ferocity. "He's not coming back, unless his spirit wants to know what we did with his bones." Here Zoose knocked on the tall beam that was holding up the silk tent, as if for luck.

Freya wasn't sure if she took his meaning.

"Nils got him with his gun," elaborated Zoose. "Sent him to the big iceberg in the sky!"

"You're telling me that the bear is dead," Freya concluded.

"Dead as a dodo. Turned into bear burgers—which happen to be quite tasty, I've discovered."

"I do hope you're joking," said Freya with a shudder. "About the bear burgers."

"Not one bit," said Zoose. "That bear was a gift from the gods, as far as the humans are concerned. They soaked his meat in salt water, and then cooked it up and ate it with some pumpernickel. They'll eat every inch of him, except for his liver. Which is barmy, since everyone knows the best part of a polar bear is the liver. Tastes just like custard!"

"Does it?" asked Freya weakly. "Just like custard, you say?"

"It does!" affirmed Zoose. "There's nothing better. Brought you back from the brink, didn't it?"

"I suppose it did," said Freya. She wasn't going to act the delicate flower now. These were desperate times, and they called for desperate measures, even if those measures included eating the liver of a bear that had almost knocked her to kingdom come.

Of course, none of this answered the question of whether Zoose was staying with her or forging ahead on his own. Freya felt an urgent need to know. "You'll probably want to eat all the bear burgers you can before you push off, right?" She tried to keep her tone light. It was just a question, not an appeal.

"I'm not pushing off any time soon," said Zoose. "I'm done in. Tired as a mouse can be. I can't even feel my whiskers." He wrapped himself in a shaggy white rug that very much resembled a polar bear, or at least a small part of its hide. Soon he was fast asleep.

Freya's own weariness washed over her like a riptide, and she slept too. On and on she slumbered. Someone fed her (Zoose) and scratched her between her shoulder blades (again, Zoose), and there was some one-sided banter about the "corking good holiday" they were having (who else but Zoose?), but she was mostly oblivious to these things. What the men were doing she hadn't the strength to even speculate. Freya heeded nothing. She didn't care. Her mind wandered far and wide, sifting through memories it hadn't visited for many years. Like the balloon that had delivered them to this place, Freya felt herself rise and fall, rise and fall, rise and fall. But then she rose and kept rising, until at length she was properly herself again. The first thing she noticed was the steadfast rhythm of Zoose's breathing, less than a foot away from her. It was the most companionable thing she had ever heard.

Later, when they were both awake, Zoose opened the flap of their tent. They listened to the sounds the ice made under the bleak light from a waning moon. It was noisy. The ice crackled and creaked and sometimes even moaned. The wind blew over and around the humps in the floe, sending packed snow crystals skittering over its surface like sand.

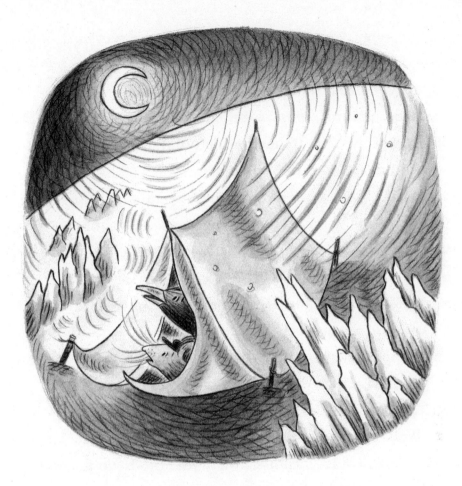

"I don't want to be out there by myself," Zoose said in the darkness of their silk cocoon. "I've had enough of that to last a lifetime. It's bad when you're with your own people and nobody wants you. When you're nothing but another mouth to feed. When the priest curses you every time you show your face. But it's worse to be alone."

"I thought the priest cursed you because you dropped your ancestors' bones into the river," remembered Freya vaguely. "Or did that come after?"

"That priest!" Zoose rolled over and spit through the opening of the tent. "That old mumbler!"

"Mumbler?" asked Freya.

"Never moved his mouth when he talked—like he was wearing a mask because no one was good enough to look at him. Oh, he was very high and mighty. His High Lordship the Mumbler."

"Priests expect a little reverence, to be sure," Freya said.

"A little reverence!" Zoose erupted with contempt and spit again. "There was this explosion of air before he said anything. 'LUH-liar!' and 'SUH-sneak thief!' and so on."

"Those aren't very nice words," said Freya.

"Well, those were the ones he was usually shouting at me," Zoose said. "I called him Uncle PUH-Peter, and he didn't appreciate it."

"The priest was your *uncle*?"

"He was my mother's oldest brother. He was in charge of blessing the sacred fish cakes, which I used to steal off the altar when nobody was looking. I couldn't see how the gods needed them more than I did—they had all the fish in the sea, while I was practically starving. Anyway, he caught on and made my mother BUH-banish me."

"Why didn't she tell him to go soak his head?" asked Freya.

"Oh, she'd never do that. Nobody would. I had dozens of aunts and uncles, and every one of them turned their backs on me. When you were CUH-cursed by the priest, that was the end of you. He said that Death would follow me wherever I went, and people believed him. Word got around for miles. They chased me out of town," said Zoose.

Freya envisioned a solitary figure, living from paw to mouth, always on the move, always alone. She imagined a young mouse who spoke only to himself, ate his meals like a fugitive and slept in vacant crooks and corners. Not even her year on the island had been as bad as that. She'd been alone, it was true, but not shunned like a plague.

"You were so awfully deserted, Zoose," said Freya. "But then you decided to visit the loneliest place on the planet. What made you do it?"

"Now, now, the North Pole could be stacked three deep with friendly people just waiting to meet us. We don't really know what it's like there, do we? Nobody does," said Zoose, looking out into the emptiness of the ice pack.

"I think we have a good idea that it's not especially crowded," said Freya softly.

It was a few minutes before Zoose spoke again. "Everyone was so happy to forget me. No, it was more than that.
They tried to erase me, see? They ousted me and turned my
name into a dirty word. My name! Zoose! It never crossed
their lips again. I didn't exist anymore. And to be honest,
I got used to not existing. But when I heard about this
balloon thing . . . I don't know. It just grabbed hold of me.
At least I will have made my mark on the world, I said to
myself, *no matter how hard they tried to blot me out.*"

"And you're sure you wouldn't rather be by yourself?"
Freya asked.

"I'd rather travel with present company, if present company will have me," said Zoose.

"Present company would be most grateful," said Freya.

And thus it was decided that (north, south, east or west)
it was better to drift together than drift apart.

CHAPTER
Seven

From the calamity of the capsized boat came the gift of a long recess, for both humans and animals. Zoose had suffered greatly from his drubbing, but things were worse for Knut. By the time the captain and Nils had dragged him out of the water, he was soaked to the skin and had come very close to losing a few of his toes to frostbite. They rubbed him all over with handfuls of coarse snow until he bellowed at them to stop, and then made him drink cup after cup of hot tea, while attempting to dry his trousers over the camp stove. But still he caught a chill, and they decided to rest until he recovered his strength.

Meanwhile, Freya and Zoose recuperated steadily. Zoose had chosen an impeccable location for their tent, set back into a natural cavity in a jagged hump of ice. Here they were well hidden from the humans and any predators.

They had food in abundance, supplementing their provisions with bear liver. As Freya convalesced, she regained a bloom that had evaporated long ago with her youth. She felt practically vivacious. For Zoose's part, he was unable to rest until he had used up the last few yards of thread sewing silk cushions for the inside of the tent.

"We're on some sort of Arctic safari!" said Freya, flustered by the profusion of pillows. But if there was a certain extravagance about this development, Freya felt Mrs. Davidson would approve. Hadn't she devoted an entire chapter to the subject of cushions and declared them a boon for an invalid with shattered nerves? *If being ambushed by a bear isn't enough to shatter one's nerves, then nothing is,* Freya thought. *Cushions are well-nigh a necessity.*

After garnishing their tent with the pillows, Zoose curled up against a pile of them and (by the looks of it) had no intention of moving any time soon. "What about your family, Freya? What were they like?" he asked.

"My family? What is there to say? In a word, we were respectable. We dressed respectably, read respectable books

and had dinner every night at five o'clock. If I had been a boy, I would have followed in Father's footsteps and dabbled in deposits."

At this, Zoose's ears pricked up. "Deposits?" he asked. "Did your people have money?"

Freya was unfazed by his bluntness. "I believe we did. We were what you might call prosperous. We had a cook and a scullery maid. A seamstress came to the house twice a year. Our carpets were shabby—Mother was always on about the carpets to Father. But he liked them the way they were. Father liked to be comfortable. As I was saying, he was in minerals. . . ."

"You said he was in finance," interrupted Zoose.

"No, I did not. Father made his money in mineral deposits, not bank deposits! He would come home at night and say that the firm had invested in a brilliant deposit of clay or salt."

"Clay or salt," repeated Zoose, sounding underwhelmed. "Was he nice, your da? Buy you candy and that sort of thing?"

"Mother didn't approve of sweets," said Freya. "But there were lots and lots of presents, especially on Christmas Eve. I never got what I really wanted, but that wasn't their fault."

"What was it you wanted?" asked Zoose, of course.

"An egg. A perfect egg that would have hatched a baby

brother or sister. How I dreamed of that egg." Freya sighed. "I'm sure I wore their ears out, begging for it. But it wasn't meant to be."

"Brothers and sisters are overrated, if you ask me. They eat your food when you're not looking and blame you when the furniture catches on fire."

"I think it would have been great fun to have a little brother," countered Freya. "Or a sister. Or one of each. However, I was an only chick, and I suppose that became the story of my life."

Zoose, who had been gnawing on some exceptionally stale bread during this chat, picked the crumbs off his homespun snowsuit and ate them one by one. "Tell me the story of your life, Freya," he said when he was done. "I could use a good yarn. Make things up, if you need to. Let's have a real potboiler!"

"Why do you think I need to embellish my history with invention to make it interesting?" asked Freya. "I might be an old maid, but that doesn't mean I've been ordinary!"

Zoose raised his eyebrows skeptically.

"There are some lurid details that might really shock you," she warned.

Zoose discovered an errant crumb and ate it without saying a word. And so, like Scheherazade of old ("Who?" asked

Zoose. "Oh, never mind," said Freya), she leaned against a silk cushion and began to speak. This was the story that unfolded over several days:

⸎

There was once a family of penguins who lived in a house far enough from the city that Mother could have apple trees and elderflower bushes. It was a brick house, whitewashed on the outside, with a vibrant red-tiled roof. It was not a small house; in fact, it was optimistically large for a family of three. Yet each room was filled with the love that the penguins had for each other. Even the formal dining room felt cozy and warm, because the meals were seasoned with joy and served with affection.

Mother was a round little bird who was famous in three counties for her wine, which she made from the fruits and flowers of her own garden. When guests sampled her rhubarb and rose petal concoction, it gave them a euphoria that lasted well into the next week. Even children were permitted to sip it by the thimble-sized cupful! Mother spent her days telling the cook what to make for dinner and reminding the maid not to polish the silverware with boot-blacking. She also took care of Baby Frey, who was her pride and joy.

Father was a taller-than-average penguin who wore a taller-than-average hat. His hat was so tall that he could stand Baby Frey on his head and cover her with it. He often snuck her out of the house this way, until Mother noticed she was missing and would march out the front door to demand Baby's return. It was remarkable how many times Mother fell for this trick—nearly every morning! Years and years later, Freya could conjure the smell of that hat: the clovey essence of Father's feather pomade.

While Freya did long for a playmate in the form of a brother or sister, her early years were full of amusements. There was nothing her parents loved more than company, and they did not lack it. Scarcely an evening went by when there wasn't a guest or two (or three or six) for dinner. Weekends were devoted to excursions with friends, often to the coast, where everyone was encouraged to shed their clothes and bathe in the wonderful, chilly waves. Mother and Father were passionate swimmers. Mother's precise, delicate strokes were much praised by observers, whereas Father went in for diving. He could stay beneath the sea for what seemed like ages, only surfacing when Mother's patience with his underwater antics was exhausted. Freya herself bobbed like a black-and-white cork, until Father taught her to zip between the waves like a two-masted clipper. To see his daughter swim boldly was Father's fondest desire, surpassed only by Mother's aspiration that she do it in style. These were their twin ambitions for Freya, who never for a second doubted that one day she would be both fearless and fashionable!

Freya's birthdays were an opportunity to fill the house and garden with every penguin from miles around. First there was the matter of the Danish flag, which Father raised on the pole as soon as the sun came up. Then came an avalanche of well-wishers, many bearing small gifts wrapped in tissue paper, for which they were rewarded with as many slices of cake as they might conveniently stuff into their beaks, washed down with glasses of Mother's wine. Naturally this sort of indulgence resulted in much singing and dancing. And Freya enjoyed it all, perched atop an extraordinary throne that Mother wove every year out of the branches of her elderflower bushes. At the setting of the sun, fire was applied to the throne, and the remaining guests stood around it in a circle, roasting marshmallows. There was nothing better in the world than a slightly charred birthday marshmallow.

One afternoon, Father came home from work early. He stood in the sunlit foyer, shifting his weight from one foot to the other in excitement. "Great news, my dear!" he called up to Mother, who hurried down the stairs to meet him. "We've bought up a pit of the finest white clay you've ever seen!" White clay was terribly important in Denmark, for without it there could be no porcelain dishes, and Denmark was known all over the world for the beauty of its porcelain.

"Oh, hurrah!" exclaimed Mother. "It's a good one, then?"

"My word, it's the richest deposit we've ever seen. Positively magnificent!" said Father. "And just on the other side of town, by the cliffs."

"Then I insist on seeing it with my own eyes," Mother said, catching the spirit of the thing. She was keenly interested in Father's ventures and had invested no small amount of her own money in his firm. "Let's take the trolley and then walk the rest of the way. I could use a good ramble."

To this Father readily agreed, and because it was some distance to the pit, they resolved to leave Baby Frey (she was not really such a baby anymore, but quite little in any case) at home with the cook, who would give her dinner and see to her bath. Thus Freya's life was spared when the side of the pit collapsed, taking Mother and Father with it.

❧

(Here, Freya paused to gauge her listener's reaction to this news. Zoose had shown a singular aversion to almost any mention of death. But, absorbed in the story, he did not even flinch at her parents' demise, so Freya carried on.)

Now, there is such a thing as a reversal of fortune. Imagine that a beggar who hasn't a penny to his name is suddenly unveiled as the long-lost crown prince of Siam! *That* would be a reversal of fortune. Or perhaps a family on the brink of starvation discovers that the spider living in their rafters has been spinning golden floss out of her backside for years and their attic is full of the stuff. What a reversal of fortune that would be!

Sadly, a reversal of fortune can also work in the other direction, and a small penguin who has known only love and gladness her entire life can lose everything in a single tragic instant. Freya was to experience a reversal like this.

The cook did her best to look after Freya in the days following Mother and Father's dreadful accident. But as is the custom in such cases, custody of the orphan (and her tidy inheritance) was granted to the nearest relative. It mattered not at all that the nearest relative had never met Freya and didn't particularly like children. It was pointless to suggest that this relative should have been forbidden from actually being in the same room as a child. The law was the law. Freya was sent to live with her father's only sister, Aunt Agatha, in Sweden.

So distraught was Freya at leaving the white house with the red roof and the apple trees and the elderflower bushes that she stopped eating. It may have seemed like a protest against the unwelcome removal from her home, but it was no such thing, for it was not in Freya's nature to demand that she be given her own way. It was simply grief. Her spirit was being dismantled, and she was unable to receive nourishment in any form. During the voyage to Sweden, Freya did something very rare for such a young penguin: she molted. Day after day her feathers fell out, until, by the time she arrived at her aunt's house, she was as bald and skinny as the day she was hatched.

She was nobody. She was nothing.

ᴄ Eight ᴄ

The shame of being as featherless as a chick was something Freya never conquered. She hadn't known shame at all until the day she arrived on her aunt's doorstep and saw herself as her aunt saw her, repulsive and puny. Then shame washed over her like a river of dark muck. Of course she was not allowed to attend school until her feathers grew back. This took many months, most of which Freya spent wrapped in a Persian blue shawl that had belonged to her mother. At last it became so tattered that Aunt Agatha had it burned.

Aunt Agatha was as selfish a penguin as ever lived. In that day and age, she was what was known as a spinster. That's not a very pleasant word, maybe, but it wasn't a very pleasant time to be old and unmarried. There were in general two directions a spinster might take. She could devote herself to the needy penguins in her neighborhood, making sure they had soup to eat, warm underclothes, and someone to listen to their troubles. If Freya's aunt had been this variety of spinster, oh, how differently things might have turned out! Sadly, she was of the second sort: tight, prudish and aloof. To recognize the needs of another penguin, let alone one who was bald and bewildered, was quite impossible. It was out of the question. It would never do.

There is some debate as to whether Agatha had ever been a child. If she had, it was not a stage that left much of an impression on her mind. To have a child show up and actually require things of her was unacceptable. She determined to put an end to that at once. It was *she* who would require things of Freya, and here is a list of those requirements:

No disorderly conduct, for that is anarchy
No profanity, audible or imagined
No balderdash or telling of puns
No cherry-flavored cough drops (only eucalyptus)
No breathing through one's mouth
No sidelong glances, for they are not to be borne
No wallowing in grief, or happiness
No unseemly books
No lewd laughter

No scratching

No birthdays

No pastels

No toys

"No school" might have easily appeared on that list, had the law allowed it.

Fortunately, it did not. With the greatest reluctance, Aunt Agatha permitted Freya to walk the four blocks to and from the large stone building where young penguins were educated.

One wishes one could say, honestly, that school was a glorious deliverance for Freya. That was not the case. It's true that she was a good student (particularly in poetry— she proved to have a sensitive understanding of this subject, and a terrific memory). But she was an odd bird, and penguins (like most creatures who walk the earth) do not like odd. A student can be annoying or silly and manage to fit in. She can even be mean and still have a friend or two. The one thing she cannot be at school is odd.

Yes, Freya was odd. She never overcame the humiliating loss of her feathers. Of course they had for the most part grown back (the thin spots on her back and shoulders were well covered by her uniform), but something was wrong. By the time penguins are old enough to go to school, their yellow feathers have come in. Beautiful golden plumes adorn their heads, often starting just above their eyes. Sometimes they crop up in obedient stripes, and sometimes they shoot out in a sensational, spiky profusion. But they are always remarkable, and everyone has them. Everyone but Freya.

"Where are your yellows?" asked her classmates, first from curiosity and later from cruel spite. "Freya's got no yellows! She looks like a baby!" was their daily observation. So Freya took to wearing a hat, indoors and out. She even wore a hat to bed. Wild horses could not drag Freya's hat off her head. It was just a matter of time before students began to call her Freyhat, and she went by this name until the day she graduated.

In the years after she finished school, Freya watched as her classmates paired off to start their own families, or opened dress shops, or became paleontologists or musicians. Some stayed on at school as teachers. One penguin, whom Freya had privately admired very much, wrote a book of poetry that won awards, both locally and abroad.

What Freya herself did was, in a word, nothing.

Perhaps "nothing" is an exaggeration. After all, she lived with Aunt Agatha as something between a companion and a servant. She kept the house tidy and prepared their meals. She sent the laundry out (but pressed and starched their collars herself). She read at night from a book of her aunt's choosing, usually a merciless compilation of wisdom from a prior century. She attended no parties, no picnics, no plays, no excursions to the seashore, and never, under any circumstances, did she go to the opera. This was easier than you might suppose, because she was never invited.

Things changed slightly when she came into her inheritance. Before that, Aunt Agatha had given her so little pocket money that she couldn't afford the fare to go downtown, let alone buy a dish of meatballs when she got there. But after her inheritance was settled, Freya took a few liberties. To begin with, she ordered a better hat. She also frequented bookstores and allowed herself an occasional purchase.

One day, through a bookseller's window, Freya spied a small text bound in leather of Persian blue, embossed in gold with words that read *"Hints to Lady Travellers at Home and Abroad,* by Mrs. L. C. Davidson." Overcome with the desire to possess this article, she rushed into the shop and acquired it immediately. It was not at all in keeping with her normal behavior, which was the opposite of impulsive. Not until much later did she recall the blue shawl that had belonged to her mother, the one that had enfolded her securely until Aunt Agatha abolished it.

Whatever the reason for her strange spontaneity, the book was the second thing that changed Freya's life forever. Travel literature written for females had become fantastically popular, but this was her first glimpse into the world of cycling tours and dress hampers and passports. She read it from cover to cover, and then again, and then once more. Every "hint" was pondered and imagined. Should one really provide each pair of shoes, boots and slippers "with a bag of its own, made of Holland linen bound round neatly with braid"? Mrs. Davidson seemed to think so. Was accident insurance a smart idea? Yes, it was, said Mrs. Davidson.

In short, Freya became obsessed with the idea of travel. She pored over train schedules, memorized exchange rates and dreamed of ocean liners. She ordered a trunk with removable trays, and a copper foot warmer covered in green wool. She practiced lighting a clever pint-sized stove in case she should have to boil a cup of water in the middle of the night at a boardinghouse where the kitchen fire had been extinguished.

But the gulf separating Freya's imaginations from real action was vast. One might think that spending a week in (let us say) Paris, munching on baguettes, would be a simple matter of buying tickets and packing a suitcase. In this, one would be completely mistaken. That is not how things were back then, and that is certainly not how things were for Freya. She had become both her aunt's custodian and her prisoner. Who would dispense Auntie's pills twice a day, if not Freya? Who would push Auntie's wheelchair up and down the street in the afternoon and then give her tea, but Freya? Who would fetch Auntie her reading glasses when she called for them? Dust the parlor? Water the violets? Society frowned upon penguins who forsook their elderly relatives for a thing as frivolous as traveling.

Then Aunt Agatha did something generous for the first time in her life: she choked on a dumpling and died.

Independence was hardly immediate. Experience is the best teacher, and Freya's experiences had taught her to do very little of her own free will. When Aunt Agatha was alive, she obeyed Aunt Agatha. Who would guide her now?

Who, indeed. Waiting in the wings, just as bossy but far more benevolent, was Mrs. Davidson. That voice, an insistent whisper for so long, grew in volume until it was a loud roar in Freya's ears. *Go forth!* said Mrs. Davidson of the Persian blue book. *Wander! Be a traveler!*

Even so, it took Freya a year to muster the resolve to leave her aunt's house. An entire year was devoted to this decision, as unimaginable as it sounds. However, when at last she assembled her luggage and had it conveyed to the port, where it would be loaded onto a steamer, Freya meant business. The *what, how* and *why* of her adventure had been endlessly debated; the *where* of it had not. There had never been a question of destination. Freya longed to go back to the white house with the red roof and the apple trees and the elderflower bushes. She would go home to Denmark.

Of course she could have sailed to Denmark directly, but that was little more than a ferry crossing, and nothing like the odyssey of her fantasies. What would a real traveler do? Mrs. Davidson had written favorably of sea voyages, and they seemed to have an element of romance that Freya had most categorically never known.

She decided to take a cruise around the archipelago of northern islands called Svalbard, famous for its rugged beauty. A cruise would allow her to see many new things from the comfort and safety of what Mrs. Davidson called "a kind of floating hotel." And after visiting the massive glaciers and exotic coastlines of Svalbard, the ship would turn south and stop at various ports of call along Norway. Freya would disembark at one of these ports and, by train and boat, travel to Denmark at her leisure.

What a lovely journey it would have been, had things gone as planned. Alas, things did not. The good ship *Angrboda,* as she was christened, sailed under a moonless sky and struck an iceberg on the sixth night of the cruise. In less than thirty minutes, she sank, taking many passengers with her. Not all passengers were trapped belowdecks when it happened. Some made it into the life rafts, including a family of gentle woodland grouse of whom Freya had become very fond. Forever after, Freya prayed they had not died of cold and fright before being rescued by a passing Norwegian whaling vessel or the like.

As for Freya, she was stupefied that something as conventional as a cruise could go so horribly awry. Didn't life owe her the smallest portion of felicity? Had she really asked for too much? She felt paralyzed, tethered to the deck chair where she had been reading under the lamplight. But this inertia was fleeting, and in due course she thrust aside her book. Tearing off her tweed traveling dress and shoes, Freya climbed onto the rail of the deck and dove into the waves. She swam with a swift current and washed up on the shore of an uninhabited island, along with two of her own trunks, including the one in which she had packed Mrs. Davidson's *Hints to Lady Travellers.* A good deal of the ship's cargo washed up as well. This godsend (consisting mainly of foodstuff, some of it very fancy) was enough to keep Freya's body and soul together. The tinned peaches and Russian caviar were first-rate. No, she did not want for sustenance—only for someone to share it with.

She didn't learn the name of the place until a month later, when Captain Andrée arrived to make his first attempt to fly a balloon to the North Pole. It was called Danskoya, and the captain and his crew failed, for the winds were not in their favor. Freya saw it all from the mouth of a cave and watched the humans pack up and leave. If they were crestfallen and even disgraced, so was she. Why hadn't she found a way to steal aboard their boat? She should have at least tried! Instead, she let fear get the upper hand, and for that she was soundly punished. She spent another year on the island, as submerged in loneliness as the *Angrboda* was submerged under the sea. She was steeped in it like a teabag, soaking it into the very bones of her body. If she had been an outcast before, now she was positively bereft.

But then the humans came back, bringing with them a new balloon, and another basket, and a stowaway named Zoose.

❧❧❧

Zoose blinked at the mention of his name, spellbound as he had been by Freya's tale. Freya looked at him strangely, for she had been in something of a storyteller's trance herself.

"So you decided to try your luck in a balloon, after all that," said Zoose.

"I was determined to have one true adventure," Freya said. "I thought, 'If I can make myself do this, my life will mean something. It won't have all been a waste. I'll become the penguin Mother and Father wanted me to be. I'll be fearless and fashionable, not frightened and forgotten!' I know it sounds silly."

Zoose scratched his chin and studied Freya's face. "Seems to me you may have become that penguin already," he said. This in itself alarmed Freya, but not nearly as much as when he reached up and plucked a feather from her head.

"Ouch!" she yelped. "What was that for?"

Zoose said nothing but held up the feather for Freya to see. And in the growing light of the new day, she saw it very well. It was as yellow as butter.

~ Nine ~

"**T**ell us another story, Freya," wheedled Zoose. "You tell a corker of a tale, you know."

"No, I do not," Freya said mildly. "A tale-teller is a person who tells falsehoods, whereas I am as honest as the day is long."

"Oh, please, Freya, *pleeeeease*," said Zoose. His reedy voice issued from the pile of cushions under which he had tunneled. The nights were growing longer, and Zoose's appetite for Freya's tales was boundless.

Freya, after many trips back to the balloon, had contrived to fill her corner of the tent with a mound of cotton batting, and now sat upon this fluffy nest like a small empress. She regarded Zoose benevolently, although it was hard to see where the pillows ended and the mouse began. Freya enjoyed being entertaining. She relished it!

"Hmmm." She pondered, lowering the flame in her portable reading lamp to its most economical level. "Let's see. Did I tell you about the time I swallowed a beakful of sea glass? It has a happy ending, although it *was* touch and go for a while."

There was a sort of muffled response from the jumble of pillows, which Freya took to be encouragement. She stretched her wings, organized her thoughts, and was about to begin when a scuffling noise outside the tent interrupted her.

"Did you hear that, Zoose?" she asked.

"Hear what?" asked Zoose from his cushy lair.

The noise repeated itself, more distinctly. Then someone cleared his (or her) throat. Freya stayed still, listening hard.

"Hello? Hello?" called a voice on the other side of the tent flap. "Is anyone home?"

Zoose popped into view immediately. He and Freya stared at each other, hardly breathing.

"Oh, dear, I've come at an inconvenient time," said the voice. It was a very melodious one, if shockingly unexpected. "I promise I'm harmless."

"Do you think they know we're in?" whispered Freya, as if an ordinary evening at home were being disrupted by a brush-and-mop salesman.

"'Course they know, whoever 'they' are," Zoose said.

"It's cold out here," the voice informed them. "Cold enough to freeze the bottom off a brass monkey! *I* would never say such a thing, on the whole. But others would!" This was followed by a low, charming laugh.

There was no help for it. Zoose squared his shoulders and pulled back the flap of the tent.

Only once in Freya's life had she gone to the theater, and she had never forgotten the thrill when the curtains were raised to reveal an actress spectacularly lit by dozens of stage candles. So it was now. Framed in the tent's entrance, resplendent in a cascade of silvery moonbeams, stood a snow fox.

Freya caught her breath in wonder. Zoose positively goggled. For a moment, they were suspended in time. The creature's face was turned demurely to the side, eyes downcast. Every star in the Arctic sky seemed to twinkle all at once, punctuating the flawlessness of her fur. She raised her head and peered into the tent. Her ears were perfect isosceles triangles. Her eyes were like black diamonds. She was blindingly beautiful.

"May I . . . ?" she murmured, as if delicacy prevented her from making too forward a request.

"Yes, of course, come in," said Freya, and the fox put two exquisite paws over the tent's threshold. Then she slipped all the way inside, curling her tail around her body with a silky flourish. Zoose, wordless for once, let the flap of the tent fall shut behind her. But for Freya's small lamp, they were quite in the dark again.

It seemed correct to wait for the fox to introduce herself, which she wasted no time in doing. "Thank you very kindly. I don't think I would have lasted much longer out there. When I saw your tent, I almost fainted. Fainted with relief! My name is Marguerite."

Freya went next. "I'm Freya from Sweden," she said. "And this is my traveling companion, Zoose. He hails from London. We're explorers, one might say. May I inquire what brings you so far north?"

"Goodness, I'm a refugee," said the fox. "Yes, some would call me that. It's a fair way of putting it. Not to bore you with the particulars."

"Oh, please, do tell us how you come to be in the middle of nowhere," urged Freya. "We'd love to know, truly we would."

"We got all the time in the world," said Zoose with an almost submissive respectfulness. "Spare no details. Life story, and all that."

There followed a long pause as the fox judged whether she should grant her audience the boon of an explanation (or so it seemed to Freya). Finally, she spoke. "I am originally from"—here she hesitated for the tiniest moment—"Poland. Are you familiar with that country? No? Well, I am most certainly from Poland. In fact, I am Countess Marguerite, although let us not stand on that formality! How silly it would be to require you to call me Countess, though I would not object if you insisted on doing so."

"'Countess Marguerite' is easy enough," said Zoose.

"I thank you for that," replied the fox, who may have nodded in a dignified sort of way, although it was too dark to be sure. "I was highly born, but I felt—I feel!—for the plight of common workers. The oppressed, one might say. Normal folks, as the expression goes. The salt of the earth."

"Bumpkins," agreed Zoose. "I know a few."

(*Bumpkins?* wondered Freya. She did not doubt that Zoose knew more than his share of bumpkins, but was flummoxed by this newcomer and the bizarre direction her tale was taking.)

"Indeed," continued Marguerite. "I fought injustice wherever I found it. I sheltered the homeless in my castle. I campaigned for women to have the vote. Do you know what the vote is? Well, I wanted women to have it. And children too! I spent my fortune buying everyone bread and shoes. In the end, the aristocracy had enough of my agitation. They kicked me out of the country! Out of Poland."

"That's foul play!" said Zoose, outraged. "Thuggery!"

"Do you mean to say," Freya probed, "that you were exiled because you clothed and fed the needy?"

"Just so," said the fox with a sniff. "They deported me to the North Pole!"

Freya pressed her beak together, but a rampant need for correctness prevailed. "You are aware that this isn't the North Pole. . . ."

"But it's close!" Zoose interrupted, as if to console Marguerite for not having been banished far enough. "Let's not stand on ceremony! It's very close!"

"And I am very tired," said the countess, yawning adorably. "I can hardly keep my eyes open. Do you have a place I could rest? Just for the night. I would never want to impose."

These words signaled that introductions were over and that it was now time to turn in. Zoose, obedient as a puppet, delved back under his pillows, but not until he'd offered the best one up for the fox's own use. Freya was a less eager host but did not want to be thought boorish by this sophisticated stranger. She moved her nest of cotton batting closer to Zoose's corner and made room for their guest. Marguerite arranged herself atop a pillow, occupying half the tent (or rather more than half) in a matter-of-fact way that did not invite discussion. Soon both she and Zoose could be heard snoring softly, leaving Freya to marvel at how quickly it had all happened.

Freya thought about the preposterous demands of foreign travel. Sharing cramped quarters with a vagrant (though quite gorgeous) fox? Who could have predicted it? Marguerite seemed genteel enough, but Freya was bothered by the invasion. It was so improbable, so sudden! On the other hand, Zoose was utterly unperturbed. *He's bewitched,* she decided as she surrendered to nervous, fitful dreams.

The next morning, Freya and Zoose gave several tender pieces of bear liver to Marguerite. She ate them up quickly, with dainty snaps of her sharp white teeth. In return, she dug into a large, spangled bag of her own and presented them with a quantity of roasted peanuts. Freya scrutinized the food with uncertainty—it did seem irregular to be carrying a stash of peanuts around on an ice floe in the middle of the Arctic Sea. And was it absolutely necessary for Zoose to make such a show of eating each and every one?

"Honestly, Zoose, one would think you'd never seen a peanut before," she ventured as he bit through another hull and harvested the contents.

"Come to Papa, you delicious thing," he said, ignoring Freya and flipping a peanut into his mouth. "And thank you, Countess. Imagine trading a piece of rubbery old liver for such a treat as this. We're taking advantage of you is what we're doing!"

Freya had to object. "You love bear liver. It tastes like custard, you said!"

"Not even custard tastes like custard when you have to eat it every day," replied Zoose.

Marguerite smiled magnanimously and then went back to licking her front right paw. Freya was compelled to notice that every so often she winced and let out a short bark of pain.

"Are you in distress, Marguerite?" she asked.

The fox nodded. "I stepped on an icicle. Nasty thing! It went right through my poor foot!"

"Oh, Freya will fix you up!" volunteered Zoose. "Freya, grab your article of whatsit! You must have something in there that will put the countess right again."

Freya duly fetched her Article of Faith and returned to Marguerite, opening it to take out a roll of clean cotton bandaging and some antiseptic cream. (Was it her imagination, or was the fox examining the contents of her pouch with a covetous fascination?) Marguerite lifted her paw, and Freya took a look—there was a small cut on the pad under one of her toes, which Freya dabbed with the cream.

"Ow!" yipped Marguerite. "Is it very bad? Am I torn all to pieces? Gashed?"

"Good grief, it's just a nick," said Freya.

"Hallelujah," breathed Zoose, sounding truly relieved. "Mind you don't leave a scar, Freya, whatever you do."

"Leave a scar? On the bottom of her foot?" Freya was peeved by his earnest solicitude toward the fox. It was wholly out of proportion to what the situation required. Zoose was overdoing it, and not by a little! She unrolled the bandaging, nettled.

"In Poland, there was nothing the court physician couldn't do," Marguerite said as Freya cut a bandage to just the right length. "He could bring a person back from the dead, nearly. He reattached the king's own tail after a hunting accident! It was a miracle. But you will do your best, I am sure."

Yes, Your Highness, I will do my humble best was what Freya almost said. But she kept this and other thoughts to herself as she wrapped the bandage tightly around the fox's paw and ankle. Then she tied the ends into a square knot and stood back.

Marguerite stretched her leg and put some weight on it. The bandage held well. She did a low arabesque, and then twirled winsomely.

"Good as new," she acknowledged.

"Even better!" added Zoose brightly.

Freya said nothing.

They spent the day on the ice floe. Zoose scampered ahead, intent upon showing Marguerite all of his favorite places. Marguerite rewarded him with gracious smiles; periodically she pricked her ears in his direction until he was almost undone by his desire to please her. Until now, Freya had been unaware that Zoose *had* any favorite places, and she lagged behind. When they reached a hummock with one side that sloped evenly to the ground, Zoose sprinted all the way to the top.

"Freya, come up here!" he called. "Show the countess that thing you do! Countess, you've got to see it! Freya can flump onto her belly and streak down the ice like a rocket! It's a real pip!"

"Oh, how comical. Flump onto her belly! I should love to see that," said Marguerite so smugly that Freya felt an actual stab of pain. Executing a perfect belly flop took a great deal of daring and technique, and Freya had both. But she would no sooner flop down the ice in front of Marguerite than fly to the moon.

"Not for all the tea in China," she said, and waddled back to the tent by herself. Zoose could play the clown for the fox all he liked, but she had better things to do. She doubted they would miss her overly much.

In the evening, Zoose and Marguerite returned, glowing from their romp across the ice. They lounged against the largest pillow and shared some peanuts with each other. They scarcely seemed to notice that Freya was there. Now she worried that she had been too touchy, and that in fact they hadn't missed her in the slightest. Was she really so dispensable? How easy it was to become the third wheel! Abashed, she offered to check the fox's bandage.

"Say, Freya, what was that story you started in on last night? The one with you swallowing glass?" asked Zoose. It was clear that he was acting under some compulsion to be amusing, lest Marguerite become bored with their company.

"Really? Am I to be storyteller as well as nurse?" asked Freya as she retied Marguerite's bandage efficiently.

"Oh, don't be like that. Nobody tells a story like you do!" said Zoose.

"I do not mind a story, myself," purred the fox. "One that suits. A befitting story, with a moral."

Marguerite's virtuous tone rankled Freya. "It was nothing. Just a silly thing I did when I was a chick. I was walking along the beach with my mother when I spied dozens of pieces of sea glass. They were so irresistibly bright and in every color—jade and turquoise and even vermilion!

I pointed them out to Mother, and she said they were mermaid tears. She warned me not to eat them. What was she thinking? Naturally, the moment she turned her back, I swallowed as many as I could!"

"No, you didn't!" exclaimed Zoose. "What happened?"

"Only what you might expect. I got a cracking bellyache, and Mother guessed what I'd done. She told Father, who held me upside down and shook me until I vomited up every last piece of glass."

Marguerite coughed and looked away in some distaste. There was a moment of awkwardness. Zoose's animated face faltered as he realized that the fox's sensibilities had been offended. *How disobliging of her,* thought Freya. *She might at least thank me for binding her paw!* Freya remembered the way the sea glass had tasted as it had lodged in her gullet, hard and cold and not unlike the feeling she had right now for Marguerite. What was the use of being beautiful if one couldn't manage a modicum of manners? It was just a story about a baby penguin, after all!

"I'd eat an entire bucket of sea glass now to be back on that beach with Mother! There's your moral!" said Freya.

"'There's your moral!'" said Marguerite, imitating Freya in an offhand way. She lowered her head between her paws and repeated it to herself with a frothy laugh, as if it were the funniest thing she'd ever heard. "'There's your moral! There's your moral!'"

That night Freya fell asleep remembering how splendid it had been to crash on an ice floe hundreds of miles away from home, with no way of knowing where she was, with nobody to come to her rescue and (most important of all) with no Marguerite.

ᘐ Ten ᘗ

Freya opened one eye just a sliver, and then squeezed it shut again. Morning had come, and Marguerite was still there, reposed against a pillow. Worse yet, she was watching her. Freya could feel it.

"Wake up, sleepyheads," cajoled the fox.

Freya lay still and willed Marguerite to leave. She'd cropped up from nowhere—couldn't she evaporate just as easily?

"Anyone for breakfast?" Marguerite asked. "A bowl of sea glass, perhaps?"

This brought a tiny snicker from Zoose's corner, and Freya went rigid with fury. It was going to be a very long day indeed if *that* was how he was going to play things.

Then Marguerite changed tactics. "Freya," she said, "I adored your story last night. Yes, I really did. I was riveted, as they say."

Freya opened both eyes. So did Zoose.

"It was very . . . informative," continued Marguerite. "I understand you so much better now. You and little Zoose."

Freya and Zoose sat up. What was she trying to tell them? Her words sounded like a preamble to something momentous. She searched their faces. Were they ready to hear what she had to say next? She bit her lip doubtfully.

Then she relented. "How you must both long to go home. What if I were to introduce you to a friend who could take you back? Safe and sound? No questions asked?"

Freya and Zoose stared at her, and then looked at each other. Their mouths hung open in confusion. "I don't understand. What is it that you're suggesting?" asked Freya.

"Oh, well, it's not complicated. I would have mentioned it last night, but I didn't want to presume," said the fox. "I have a friend, you see—an ally. He's a whale. Do you know what a whale is? Because, as I say, he is one. A whale."

"Of course we know what whales are," said Freya, who had seen many whales in her life but had never been closely associated with any. "I fail to see how a whale will get us off the ice."

"You could ride on his back," said Marguerite. "It would be child's play! So easy! And he'd be happy to do it. He could take you to the coast of Sweden, and you could each make your way home from there." She explained this with exaggerated patience, as if they were simpletons.

"Why doesn't he take *you* home?" Freya asked, unable to help herself.

Marguerite sighed with regret. "Impossible. I'm far too famous. I'm recognized everywhere I turn. No, the Defendress of the Friendless can never go home. She has nowhere to lay her head. Nowhere at all."

Freya was overcome by an intense dislike for the fox, who struck her as more deluded by the minute. Far too famous, indeed! Freya was having none of it. "I need some air," she fumed, and left the tent.

Then Marguerite confessed her own dedication to "daily conditioning" and followed Freya, jostling her just a little as she swept by. The fox sashayed over the ice, back arched, hips sublime (yet tasteful)—the very picture of refinement.

Freya spun around and glared at Zoose, who was half in and half out of the tent. He unshelled a peanut absently while contemplating Marguerite's disappearing form. Freya couldn't take it for one more minute.

"Defendress of the Friendless?" she spluttered. "I have never heard anything so ludicrous in all my life, and neither have you."

"You've really gone off your onion," said Zoose, chewing slowly.

"Just try and say it ten times fast!" said Freya.

"What difference would *that* make? Give the countess a chance," said Zoose.

Freya felt the cold sea glass in her throat and wondered if she might gag. "If she's a countess from Poland, then I'm the queen of Sheba! You're an easy mark, Zoose, you know that? A really easy mark!"

"I don't know what you mean," said Zoose.

"Yes, you do," said Freya. She bustled back inside and picked up all the peanut shells she could find. Then she flung them out the front of the tent, peppering Zoose when he didn't duck fast enough. Everything was topsy-turvy now, and Freya blamed the fox for that. She didn't trust her one iota. No, not one whit, jot or tittle! But neither did

Freya trust herself. Hadn't she misjudged people and situations before? Made great errors? Miscalculated badly? She had.

Be that as it may, she said to herself, *this smells more of fish than of whale. I must be careful.*

Accordingly, when the fox returned to the tent and renewed her proposal, Freya was on guard. "Would you care to meet my special friend? My comrade? I am sure he would like to meet you," Marguerite persevered. Mulish and unbending, Freya folded and refolded a spare cardigan as if her life depended on it, and kept her beak shut.

It was a different matter with Zoose, however. "Why, I'd like that very much," he said, dismissing Freya's cluck of disapproval. "Any friend of yours is a friend of mine!"

At this, Marguerite bestowed a dazzling smile on Zoose and turned on her heels, trotting away from the campsite. Zoose followed her, and Freya (refusing to be left out, come what may) followed Zoose. The fox was soon ahead of them both.

"This won't end well," said Freya as they struggled to keep up with Marguerite's brisk pace. "Mark my words, it won't."

"You've got a little bee under your bonnet," observed Zoose, panting. "But what's the harm in giving her the benefit of the doubt? The countess seems like a good sort to me."

"Please do me the favor of not referring to her as the countess, or I might laugh my head off," said Freya, puffing and wheezing.

"Oh, so you know what a countess looks like?" challenged Zoose between gulps of air. "Why are you so sure she's not who she says she is?"

"Call it penguin intuition if you like. I know when I'm being bamboozled!"

"Do you?" he asked. "Because what I see here is a lady who was wronged, who isn't letting her rank, or as some might say her noble birth, get in the way of helping the likes of us!"

Freya was livid. "The likes of *us*? A lady who was *wronged*? Far be it from me to dash the cup of joy from your lips, Zoose, but she's hoodwinked you from start to finish!"

Half an hour and many differences of opinion later, Freya and Zoose joined Marguerite at the edge of the ice floe. After studying the open water, the fox put her bandaged foot up to her muzzle and issued a shrill whistle. Then she whistled a second time, and then a third. They waited mutely. Nothing appeared to be happening.

"He hears me," said Marguerite. "We have a perfect understanding, he and I. You'll see."

Freya turned to Zoose, rolling her eyes in vindication. But Zoose wasn't looking at Freya. He was looking very intently at the sea. Freya turned back and looked with him. Then she gasped in amazement. "Well, knock me over with a feather," she said. A wave had swelled the surface of the water and was coming straight at them. Then it stopped, and from the slate-colored depths a massive form arose—a great, dripping, zeppelin-shaped animal who looked for all the world like a whale!

Water sluiced off its mottled back in great rivulets, churning around its body. The sea bubbled and boiled, and steam rose in vaporous sheets from its skin. Then it reared its head to display a horn, ten feet long and fearsome, growing from its upper lip like a bayonet. Or so it seemed to Freya and Zoose.

"What *are* you?" blurted Zoose, agog.

"You're a narwhal," said Freya at almost the same moment. She had only read about narwhals in books, never imagining that they actually existed. "You're the unicorn of the sea."

This amused the whale, whose laugh sounded like

a tidal wave breaking against rocky cliffs. It regarded them first with one enormous wet eye, and then with the other. In return, they sized up the narwhal. Their prolonged examination made Marguerite impatient, and she tapped her bandaged paw against the ice. "Introductions, please," she said. "That's what happens first. Then the rest."

Zoose began. "Hello! The name's Zoose, and I'm—"

"This is the mouse," interrupted Marguerite. "His name is Zoose. And the penguin goes by Freya."

Goes by Freya? thought Freya. *Gah! If it's not one thing with this fox, it's another!* But already she could feel her resistance to Marguerite crumbling. The fox had said they would meet a whale, and here they were, meeting a whale. And not just any whale, but a narwhal! It wasn't every day one met a narwhal. In fact, it was never. "May we know what to call you?" she asked.

"Aarne. Like my father, and his father, and his father. We are always Aaaaaaaarne." His voice boomed like a kettledrum and sent ripples across the water.

"Well met, Aarne, son of Aarne," said Freya in her most correct manner.

There was a sense of expectation hanging in the air,

somehow cultivated by Marguerite. "Aarne is my very dear friend," she said, fluttering her long lashes and gazing ardently at the whale. He reciprocated her devotion fully, spraying affectionate jets of water at her from his blowhole. "We've been through many things together. We've had our times!"

At this, the whale sank under the water and then resurfaced with a monstrous swoosh, his horn extended toward the fox. She slipped her spangled bag off her shoulders and let it fall to the ice. Then she sprang onto the tip of Aarne's horn and, with the agility of a tightrope walker, pranced down its length. The whale launched her into the air, where she somersaulted once and landed on the back of his head, as light as whipped cream. She pirouetted on a hind leg until she was facing Freya and Zoose, although she looked past them, far into the distance.

Solemnly, Aarne swam away from the edge of the ice floe. His head never dipped below the surface of the sea, and Marguerite looked as if she were skimming over a plate of dark glass. Aarne began to pick up speed, but the fox never lost her footing. She was a statue of marble, the figure on the prow of a ship, an Olympian demigod, a winged angel. She was . . .

"Holy smoke, she's an acrobat," said Zoose, breaking into Freya's reverie.

Freya glanced at Zoose, noting a slow but palpable change come over him. His look of doting infatuation was being supplanted by a bitter sneer, and she didn't know which she liked less. "She's a what?" asked Freya.

"An acrobat," he said. His tone was oddly cynical. "Not your garden-variety acrobat—I'll give her that. But she's an acrobat. She'll do tricks next. Keep watching."

Now the whale and Marguerite were well away from where they had started, perhaps three hundred yards. They made a wide turn and came back, rocketing forward so fast that it seemed likely they would ram the ice floe. Freya and Zoose instinctively retreated, but Aarne veered at the last minute, sending up a sheet of frigid water that splashed the ice at their feet. Again he swam away, turning and turning in an immense ring at such a breakneck speed that he began to create a whirlpool. Still, Marguerite never bobbled or floundered. Her poise was absolute.

Freya was mesmerized by the performance. "How could I ever have thought she was trying to deceive us? She's just so . . . so . . . What is the word, Zoose?"

"So bogus?" prompted Zoose.

"So stately! So regal! I've never seen anything like it," she said in wonder. "How does she keep from falling off?"

"How? She's done it ten thousand times, that's how. Boy, I've been a chump before, but this really takes the biscuit. You were right, Freya—I've been hoodwinked!"

"About that . . . ," said Freya, her eyes glued to the exhibition in front of her. "I spoke in haste, Zoose. I'm quite embarrassed. I'm afraid I slandered Marguerite unforgivably. We'll do just as you advised and give her the benefit of the doubt."

"That we *won't*," Zoose said stubbornly. "Your hunch was spot-on, Freya. I'm the one who needs his noggin examined. The fox is a fake."

"Fake, my flippers!" Freya protested. "She has the self-command of a prima ballerina!"

"Good gravy, she's exactly like one of them bareback riders who juggle while their horse flounces around the ring. Haven't you ever been to the circus?" asked Zoose.

"I should say not!" replied Freya.

"Well, I have. I worked a circus ring in Liverpool when I was a young buck, stringing up the trapeze wires," said Zoose, fumbling with something on the ground. "Trust me, I know a circus act when I see one. And I've seen a million."

"No mere circus act could be as amazing as this. Oh, now she's standing up on two legs. What an artiste! Can you believe it, Zoose?" Zoose made no response. "Zoose? *Zoose!* What in heaven's name are you doing?"

To Freya's horror, Zoose had plunged headfirst into Marguerite's bag. All that could be seen of him were his hindquarters wriggling this way and that as Freya hissed at him to stop his madness and come out at once.

"Zoose!" she scolded. "One does not inspect the contents of a lady's purse without her express permission! It just isn't done!"

"Lady? She's no lady." Zoose emerged from the bag and wrinkled his nose with scorn.

"I beg your pardon?" asked Freya. "Were you not as recently as an hour ago calling her the Lady Who Was Wronged?"

"Yeah. That was before I found this." With a tremendous effort, Zoose pulled out a collapsible brass telescope, slim and well crafted. It was longer than he was. Standing it upright on the ice, Zoose swiveled it around so that Freya could make out the letters engraved in the bright metal. She tilted her head to the side and read them out loud: S. A. Andrée.

CHAPTER

~⚬ Eleven ⚬~

Freya was aghast. "There could be a perfectly reasonable explanation for why she has Captain Andrée's telescope," she argued. "The humans might have dropped it.
They've shed plenty of their equipment. Scads and scads of
equipment, all over the place. Perhaps Marguerite tripped
over it."

"Flapdoodle, and you know it," Zoose said.

"Put it back before they catch us poking around in her
things!" beseeched Freya.

"Her things!" scoffed Zoose. But Freya lifted the edge of

the bag, and Zoose slid Captain Andrée's telescope inside.

"I should have seen this coming," Zoose continued, mostly to himself, as he and Freya watched the fox and the whale racing around in their circle. Sure enough, Marguerite was now doing backflips. "If something seems too good to be true, you can bet your sister's sweet stockings that it is. You were right about her. She's a hustler."

"I never said she was a hustler. I don't even know what a hustler is," said Freya.

"A hustler is a con artist," said Zoose. Freya gave him a blank look. "Someone who cheats other people. A swindler. A tramp."

"Hang on, didn't *you* used to be a tramp?" asked Freya.

"Exactly! That's why I know what I'm talking about," said Zoose.

"All this just because she reminds you of someone you met at the circus. That is the worst sort of prejudice!" insisted Freya. "And why would the countess need to cheat us out of anything?"

Zoose looked at Freya as if she'd lost her mind. "Did you just call her the countess? Has your brain gone on vacation? You were sure humming a different tune this morning!"

"As were you! I simply think, you know, innocent until

proven guilty, and all that," said Freya. She wasn't quite able to look Zoose in the eye.

Zoose turned back to the sea. "And *I'm* the easy mark?"

Marguerite and Aarne were moving more deliberately now, and soon the whale stopped at the edge of the ice. Marguerite slid down his horn like a ray of light and hit the ground on all four paws. She took a bow that impressed Freya as altogether spontaneous. Aarne lingered for a minute, and then sank noiselessly back into the deep.

"That was electrifying," said Freya. Her mind was still reeling from the discovery of the telescope, but she couldn't help gushing about Marguerite's astounding demonstration.

"Yeah, first-class entertainment," said Zoose flatly. "You really stuck that landing."

Marguerite laughed her mellifluous laugh. "Oh, in Poland all the schoolchildren learn these things. In Poland, we're literally raised in the water!"

"Oh, are you? Literally?" asked Zoose.

"Yes, from the time we're pups!" insisted Marguerite.

"You must be tired, Marguerite," said Freya. She wanted Zoose to stop talking and give her time to think. "Why don't we see what we can do for lunch?"

Marguerite needed no urging. Without pausing to check her

direction, she picked up her bag and trotted toward the tent.

"Look at her go—she knows this ice floe like the back of her paw," said Zoose. "If she was ever lost, I'll eat my own hat." He scampered after the fox as fast as his little legs could carry him.

Freya didn't argue. She was beginning to feel very unhappy again. She waddled behind Zoose, trying to understand things. *What if Marguerite's story is true?* Freya wondered. *After all, Zoose can take a very dim view of things. But let's say they're both right. Why can't a Polish countess who's been banished for her political zeal also be a circus performer closely connected with a narwhal?*

A countess *could* be an acrobat. Of course she could! It sounded far-fetched—there was no escaping that fact—but Freya very desperately wished it to be true. Why was she in such a muddle?

"Let me think! Let me think!" she said out loud.

When she'd suspected Marguerite of aggrandizing her past, it had galled her. When Marguerite had claimed to have a friend who was a whale, Freya had practically ridiculed her to her face! But Marguerite *did* have a friend who was a whale, and she rode him magnificently, and didn't that put a fresh gloss on things? Didn't it give her story the teensiest ring of truth?

The teensiest ring of truth? Freya mused. *Why, I want to buy everything she's said, hook, line and sinker. What is wrong with me?*

Then an image that had been struggling for release burst into full flower. Lucid and unmistakable, Freya saw herself standing on top of the whale, just like Marguerite. She watched as she was carried like a queen (like a queen!) over the ocean and all the way back to Sweden, stepping off the head of a narwhal to the gasps of an admiring public, who would remember the sight for the rest of their lives.

In a nutshell, Freya wanted not just to go home, but to go home in a blaze of glory! That was the unvarnished reality of it. People would look at her and know that she was fearless, fashionable and all the things Baby Frey was supposed to grow up and become! She would go home as her true self.

Freya comprehended this longing deep in her heart. She grasped it fully, and she was not the least bit ashamed. If Marguerite was telling the truth, Freya would cross the ocean atop a whale, unsinkable, a traveler for the ages. And Zoose, her celebrated companion, would become simply notorious! Perhaps Mrs. Davidson would ask them both to tea.

Of course, they weren't going home atop anything if Marguerite was deceiving them, and then what to do? Regarding liars, Mrs. Davidson had no direct counsel, but she wouldn't put up with them, surely. No, no—telling lies was impolite, and on *that* topic Mrs. Davidson had plenty of advice. Regarding "uncalled-for breaches of polite-ness," Mrs. Davidson recommended a stern rebuke. *A remonstrance will often have a good effect,* she had written.

A remonstrance it would be, then, if Marguerite was lying! A frank and forthright scolding! (If that didn't work, Mrs. Davidson proposed informing the guard, which was not very practical at the moment.)

Marguerite and Zoose arrived at camp long before Freya. Zoose had left the flap open, and Freya stepped through it to find Marguerite reclining against the pile of white cotton batting that had, until now, been Freya's personal domain. So unnerved by this trespass was Freya that she moved to the farthest corner of the tent and huddled under a scrap of balloon silk.

Zoose sat on his pillows, watching Marguerite like a hawk. She offered him a peanut, which he declined stiffly. The atmosphere felt uneasy, and only became more so as the long afternoon hours resolved into an interminable evening. Freya passed the time sorting what might be true from what was arguably false. She also formulated several sting-ing remonstrances, should Marguerite be found a liar. But mostly she was miserable. How had one night with Margue-rite become three? She sensed Zoose's rancor from across the tent, and it compounded her misgivings. What could she do to rid them of this meddlesome fox?

In the morning, after eating a copious amount of bear liver, Marguerite groomed her pelt until it shone pearlescent in the early light. Then her gaze fell on Freya.

"Ah, Freya," she purred, "what do you say we girls take a little stroll? I am suffocating in here." She stood up and sauntered out of the tent. Freya looked at Zoose, who wore a gruff and unyielding expression that she had never seen before. She shrugged and followed the fox until they had gone some distance. Neither spoke as they picked their way around the cracks and ridges in the ice. Finally, Marguerite broke the silence.

"How I long to return to Poland and continue the fight to build hospitals for my people," she said.

"I understood you were fighting to give everyone the vote," said Freya.

"Well, how can people vote when they are so sick?" coun-tered Marguerite. Then she changed the subject abruptly. "Aarne says that there are humans on this ice floe.

Humans! Were you aware of that? I had no idea."

Freya thought of the captain's telescope hidden in Marguerite's bag and felt the feathers stand up on the back of her neck. The fox *was* lying! No idea that there were humans on the ice floe? A bald-faced whopper! This was the very moment for a strongly worded remonstrance, à la Mrs. Davidson. Yet Freya found that her tongue was tied.

"Aarne would dearly love to meet them. He has a great admiration for humans, you know. Some of his best friends are humans," Marguerite persisted. "Don't you think they would like to meet Aarne?"

"I—I—I couldn't possibly say," stammered Freya. She had a sudden and clear recollection of Aarne's tusk, which he could thrust ten feet over the ice with the greatest of ease. If Marguerite lured Captain Andrée and his crew close enough to the edge of the ice, Aarne could pick them off like ducks in a row. Freya suspected the whale didn't have any particular admiration for humans at all. Her blood felt very cold in her veins, and she tried to keep her breathing even.

"And these humans must have so many things to eat! Crates of food, and other things too!" Marguerite said.

Freya registered the note of greed in her voice, tinged with malice. The men *did* have crates of supplies, which any animal might consider a stupendous bounty, especially if that animal had the ice floe all to herself. Freya had a vision of being dumped, with Zoose, in the middle of the ocean by a whale whose only objective was to get back to his dearest Marguerite as quickly as possible.

So many images competed for Freya's attention that she could hardly see straight, but this much was clear: Zoose had it right. Marguerite was not a countess from Poland or from anywhere else. She was a hustler, and a dangerous one at that.

"I'd like to go back to the tent now," said Freya. "Too much excitement for one morning. And I should probably have another look at your foot."

"But of course!" agreed Marguerite.

When they reached the tent, Freya found her Article of Faith and, for lack of something better to do, prepared a new bandage. Zoose was still on his pillows. "Have a nice walk, Countess? Gather much intelligence? Reconnoiter with anyone?"

Marguerite gave one of her silvery laughs. "If I didn't know better, little Zoose, I would think you were accusing me of something. You! Accusing me!" She had opened her bag and was rummaging around inside it.

"Looking for this?" asked Zoose. He hopped off his pillows and kicked them aside, revealing the bright gleam of the telescope. Each animal eyed it as if transfixed. Then Freya realized that a remonstrance didn't actually have to include words, and she edged closer to Zoose until they stood together. The air inside the tent vibrated with tension.

"You can't stay here, Marguerite. There's a world of ice out there. You need to move along," said Zoose.

"Maybe it is you who need to move along," said Marguerite coolly. "You and the penguin."

"Nope. We were here first. Plus, there are two of us and only one of you." Zoose puffed up his chest. He looked ferocious, and his math was unassailable. "You leave. We stay."

"We only wish you well," said Freya, finding her voice before things grew any uglier. She also took the precaution of fluffing her feathers, projecting as much size and moxie as she could. "No hard feelings. Take what you need and go."

The fox put a paw on the telescope.

"Not that," said Zoose, for whom (it was possible) there *were* some hard feelings.

Marguerite saw how this would end. She took her paw off the telescope, tossed her head and flashed her jet-black eyes. Had there ever been an animal who looked so triumphant in defeat? She plucked Freya's Article of Faith off the floor with her teeth, dropping it into her bag as if it had never belonged to anyone else.

Freya sorely deplored the loss of the zippered pouch, but sweetened the deal with the rest of the tinned fish from her own supplies. It seemed a small price to pay if the fox would go away.

They waited as Marguerite adjusted the bag over her shoulders. Then the animals left the tent. Not a word was spoken as they retraced their steps across the ice floe. The penguin and mouse stopped well before the edge of the ice, but the fox went right up to the water's brink, where she paused. There was something inexpressibly lovely about her in that moment, and defiant.

"You will miss me when I'm gone," Marguerite said. "But I will not miss you. I have Aarne. I have always had Aarne." She pierced the still, cold air with three whistles. Soon the immense bulk of the narwhal appeared, and without another word she leapt onto his head. They swam away. She never looked back.

Freya and Zoose stood there for a very long time, watching as the fox and whale became smaller and smaller against the horizon. "I don't think we'll see them again," said Freya.

"Not if we're lucky," said Zoose. "Hustlers are bad business, especially the pretty ones. She would have found a way to get rid of us, and then made herself right at home."

"She would have wreaked havoc on the humans too,"

said Freya. "I gave her our last tins of smoked kippers. I hope you don't mind."

"Ah, well, smoking's bad for you," Zoose said. "By the way, she made off with your purple scarf."

"What? The thief!" cried Freya. It was a trivial offense in the grand scheme of things, but she had liked that scarf very much. The ferment of emotions she had endured over the last few days dwindled away until one thing was left: indignation. Freya was in a snit. "I've never taken anything that didn't belong to me in my entire life! Not so much as a pin or a penny! Nary a nail head! How many can make that claim, I wonder?"

"I sure can't. At least not with a straight face." Zoose smiled. It made him very happy to see Freya in top form again. "Oh, I got you something," he added, and reaching into his jacket, he pulled out the scarf he'd stolen back from the fox.

~ Twelve ~

Over the next several weeks, Freya and Zoose achieved a level of domestic tranquility that neither of them had ever known. They fell into all sorts of routines, the kind that help someone overlook the fact that he or she is floating on ice in the middle of the Arctic Sea. There was a regularity to their days that gave them comfort, and it started with breakfast.

Certainly it was not the sort of meal that would have satisfied them in their former lives, but Freya had learned a thing or two in her year on the island, which now came in very handy. From tin canteens that she kept close to her

body day and night, she poured water into a collapsible cup (hers) and a discarded mustard pot (his). To this they added some dried, crumbled algae and, after swirling it around two or three times, sipped it very slowly. Then Zoose harvested ice crystals to replenish the canteens, which Freya tucked back underneath her vest. The warmth of her body melted the ice into fresh water for their afternoon tea (which very much resembled breakfast).

Next, they tidied their tent. Freya turned her sleeping
bag inside out to air it properly, and Zoose plumped up their
pillows with many thumpings. They unpacked every bag
and bundle, taking inventory of their supplies of handker-
chiefs and quinine tablets (hers) and cheese rinds and bread
crusts (his), and what they called the larder (tinned meats
and cocoa powder and the like). Then they repacked everything very neatly.

Freya made observations in the waterproof notebook that hung around her neck, itemizing all reductions to the inventory. She also documented the weather as scientifically as she could. With no thermostat, her measurements ran the gamut from "tolerably cold" to "unreasonable" to "barbaric." Then she noted their moods, which ranged from "amiable" to "plagued with self-doubt, must get over it."

Then they attended to their personal grooming. Zoose dipped into their ample supply of bear grease and combed his whiskers until they glistened. He wrapped his head with strips of balloon silk, constructing a magnificent turban as big as a cabbage, almost. It kept his brains warm, was how he justified it to Freya. Finally, he buffed his buttons and his shoes with more grease until he looked absurdly prosperous.

For her part, Freya inspected her scarf for holes, mending them as they appeared and looping it back around her neck. Having come so close to losing it to Marguerite, the scarf was now her most treasured accessory. (Moreover, it had proved instrumental when Freya and Zoose returned Captain Andrée's telescope. The device was too heavy for either of them to convey on their own, and the difference in their heights made sharing the load difficult. They waited until the men left camp in pursuit of a walrus and then maneuvered the telescope onto the scarf. After that, it was so easy for Freya to drag it over the ice that Zoose straddled the thing like a cowboy and rode along. "Crikey, this is fun!" he whooped. "Shhh," said Freya affably. Then she towed the telescope—and its subdued passenger—to the entrance of the men's tent, where they left it.)

Freya was no stranger to bear grease either, using it to polish her orange beak, which she had always felt was her one fine feature. She fluffed the feathers on her head with pride, for she had looked at her own reflection in a pool of meltwater and counted her yellows. She had dozens of them—an embarrassment of riches. It was almost ridiculous how thickly they had grown in, as if to make up for lost time. Freya cherished every single one of them.

When their morning rituals were complete, they indulged in their daily recreation, which consisted mainly of watching the humans. This they did from behind a large, pockmarked

embankment of ice, which screened them from view while providing many peepholes.

"What are they up to now?" asked Zoose, his face pressed against one such opening.

Freya gazed through another chink, wondering the same thing. Nils and Knut were unusually active, striding across the ice field surrounding their tent with real purpose. Close to camp was a thicket of frozen slabs of ice, some set almost perpendicular to the ground and resembling oblong stalagmites. When one of the men found one they liked, they took a hatchet to it, hewing its sides straight and smooth until it resembled a large brick.

"Ah-ha," said Freya after some time. "Very sensible indeed."

"What's sensible?" asked Zoose.

"They're settling in for the winter," answered Freya. "They're making a house. Look how they shape the ice into building blocks."

As soon as she said it, Zoose saw that she was right. Nils and Knut made brick after brick, lugging each one to a flattish area by their tent and setting it into a wall. Over the days this wall grew larger and rounded. Then it became two, and finally four curved walls.

Every so often they would stop making bricks and stir up a slurry of snow and water. "And now the mortar," said Freya approvingly as they poured the mixture over the walls and waited for it to turn to solid ice. They even constructed

a secondary room, dragging the carcass of a walrus inside as soon as the walls were shoulder high, protecting the meat from marauding polar bears.

Before moving crates and photographic equipment into the house, they took pains to contour a vaulted ceiling out of ice. It was surprisingly elegant for something made of little more than frozen water and cunning. The entire structure was luminous, glowing from within as if lit by candles. Of course this was just the sun shining through the roof and refracting off the snow and ice, but it was a thing of uncommon beauty. Nils took a picture of their handiwork, with Knut striking a jaunty pose by the front opening. Freya could not resist the urge to clap her wings against her body, a penguin's salute of honor.

"Steady on," said Zoose, grinning at her sincerity.

"I'm just so proud of them," she replied. "See how they never give up?" She saluted them again.

The captain did not contribute to the ice house enterprise. His efforts were focused mainly on taking astronomical measurements to determine how far the floe had "sailed" and in what direction. He also hunted. "Yesterday we sailed two miles southwest!" he announced to Nils and Knut before picking up his rifle and striding away from camp.

"Never mind that we need to sail southeast," muttered Nils as soon as the captain was out of earshot. But Freya and Zoose heard him.

There was much excitement two days later when, incredibly, Captain Andrée sighted land. He called for Nils and Knut to join him on the edge of the floe. They passed his telescope (the very one filched by Marguerite) back and forth as they studied the hazy formation through its lens.

"It is almost certainly White Island," decided the captain, unrolling one of his maps and tracing the line of a coast with his finger. "I make it at six miles away."

"That's all? We can row there before the sun goes down!" said Nils. "I'll pack the boat!"

The captain shook his head. "Let's not be hasty. Look at those cliffs—it's a glacier! There's no place for us to put ashore. And we're actually warmer on the ice, surrounded as we are by water. Plus, at the rate we're sailing south, we'll soon encounter fish and other food from the ocean."

Knut sank down on a crate and put his wind-blistered face into his hands. Nils stared at the captain in disbelief. "This is madness! We must at least make the attempt."

Captain Andrée shook his head again. "No, no. We stand to gain little and might possibly lose everything. We shall continue to sail south."

"I beg you to stop calling it sailing!" said Nils with resentment. "We're doing nothing of the sort. Mollusks pilot these waters better than we do!"

That night the humans were silent as they ate their dinner and withdrew into the ice house. A gloomy spirit pervaded the camp, reaching its wretched fingers all the way into the silk tent, where Freya and Zoose shivered.

"What baffles me is why they stick with him," said Zoose from underneath a pile of pillows. "If the captain figures to stay behind, let him. But if the young ones want to chance it, why shouldn't they take the boat to the island?"

Freya's mind was just as troubled as Zoose's. "Well, they're obligated to each other, aren't they? They did agree to be a team when they set off together. And now to abandon the captain because of a conflict over strategy . . ." Her voice trailed off.

"But say he's wrong and they're right," argued Zoose. "Every mouse for himself, is what I think. Beast or bird, everyone is on his own at the end of the day."

"I don't know about that," whispered Freya, pulling her sleeping bag over her head.

The next day the ice floe moved closer to the island, and the next, and the next. It also moved eastward, and through the telescope the humans could see a stretch of rocky beach where a boat might land. When they were just two miles away, Nils became consumed with the desire to leave the ice pack and pleaded with Captain Andrée to reconsider. The captain was unpersuaded and remained firm in his resolve to stay put. Knut said nothing, but stood on the edge of the ice and looked over the water for hours.

That night, sleep was slow to come to Freya and brought her no rest when it did. She dreamed she sat at a table with the parish priest, who, between massive bites of rice pudding, pronounced a verse of Scripture. "Stay on the path the Lord your God has commanded you, that you may live and that it may be well with you," he droned, lowering his immense face to Freya's until they almost touched. "Be a good little chick and pass the cream," he said into her ear. Next to him sat Aunt Agatha, nodding piously. No, that wasn't it at all. Aunt Agatha sat on *top* of Freya, and they were in the ocean, and Freya was sinking beneath the salty waves. She could not liberate herself, no matter how she twisted and bucked. Down she went, farther and farther, until she hit the bottom with a shuddering crack that jolted her wide awake.

And not just her. Zoose, too, was awake and on his feet, breathing hard. Then came another crack so loud it felt as if it came from within the tent. They scrambled outside just as a third crack ripped through the air. The ice pack seemed to be shivering.

"We're breaking apart!" cried Zoose. "The ice is splitting!"

That's exactly what's happening, thought Freya. She'd seen pieces of ice splinter off packs before, crashing into other floes and buckling with prodigious force. She raced toward the humans' camp, Zoose close behind her, and together they watched in horror as a rift opened up right underneath the ice house. With a fourth deafening crack, the floe shattered and half of what had been the ice house floor floated away, spilling precious supplies and equipment into the water.

The humans, who had also been wakened by the terrible noises, watched the disaster unfold from a short distance away. Now they went into a sort of frenzy. Nils used oars and hooks to drag things back onto the floe. Knut emptied the half of the house that was still standing over solid ice. Captain Andrée righted the boat, which, tilted on its side, had served as a windbreak.

"Men, it seems we must make for the island or perish!" he said.

"Agreed!" replied Nils.

Knut picked up a bundle of canvas and stashed it in the bottom of the boat. Together the men filled the craft with as much material as they could, leaving just enough room for themselves. Then they climbed in and pushed off the side of the floe, paddling for all they were worth.

Freya turned to Zoose. "We'll follow them, of course."

"Nothing doing," said Zoose. "I'm not getting in that water, no way, no how." His voice trembled with fear.

"We're going to that island," she insisted. "How long do you think we'll last on this ice pack? It's disintegrating. You'll wind up in the water one way or another."

Zoose shook his head and wrapped his arms around himself, clamping his eyes shut.

"Look, I'll swim us there. All you need to do is keep hold of my jacket and kick your legs. It won't be pleasant, but I assure you the alternative is . . ." Freya broke off and squinted at what seemed like an extremely vast expanse of ocean. She could barely make out the edge of the island in the thin light of the rising sun. As a matter of fact, she had no idea if she could swim that far. But she would never, never, *never* let fear bully her into staying behind again. "We have no choice, Zoose. Jump in, or I'll push you."

"I won't go, I say!" shrieked Zoose. "Who died and made you queen of England? Leave me alone, or you'll regret it!"

Freya looked at Zoose, stunned. "What is wrong with you?" she said, blinking back the tears that stung her eyes.

"Oh, I'm sorry, Freya. Sorry! Sorry!" babbled Zoose, instantly remorseful. "I didn't mean that, not one bit. But I can't do it. Never could. I'll drag us both down. No, Freya, you go. I'll stay here and take my chances."

"Chances? Your chances are zero, as well you know!" said Freya. She was beside herself with desperation. How could she persuade him to get in the water when he was so far beyond reason? Then she spied a crate marked *Gingersnaps* that the humans had left behind, and she had her answer.

"Help me empty this thing," she said. "You're not going in the water—you're going over it!"

As the words left her beak, another electrifying crack reverberated like a pistol shot, and Zoose sprang into action. He spilled tins of gingersnap cookies onto the snow while Freya tossed their things out of the tent and rolled it up. Then they packed the crate to the brim and pushed it to the edge of the ice. Uncoiling a piece of rope the humans had left behind, Freya and Zoose wrapped it around the sides of the crate and knotted it fast. From the foot or so left over, they rigged a sort of harness.

"Think it'll float?" asked Zoose, climbing to the top and facing forward. He clutched the edge of the crate so tightly his knuckles popped.

"It's at least as seaworthy as I am," said Freya. She had already removed her boots, scarf, jacket, and dress, knowing how little they would serve her in the coming test.

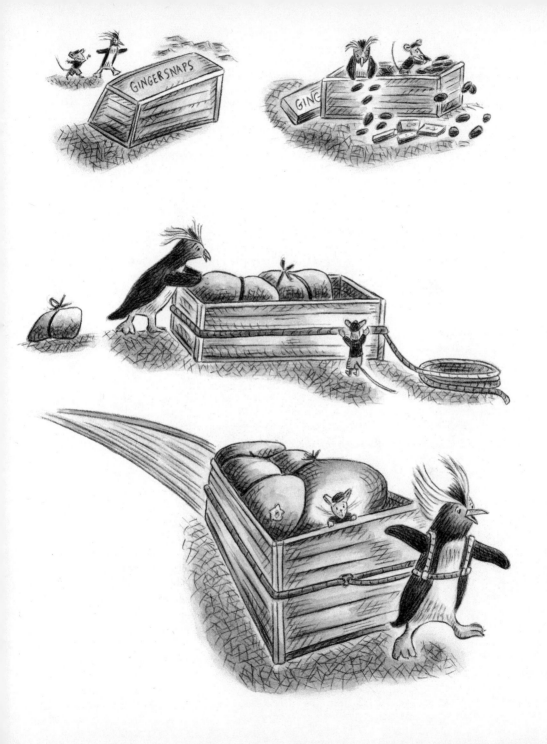

Putting her head and shoulders through the harness, she pulled the crate into the water, where it wobbled from side to side while Zoose rearranged its contents. Finally, it felt steady, and then Freya was off, swimming as she had never swum before.

If once Freya had yearned to be a fearless and fashionable bird, that dream lost its hold upon her irrevocably. She had not gone far before she realized that failure was a genuine possibility, that a desire to give up would attend each and

every stroke. Rank fear suffused her, as real as the salt in the water. She could taste it. She could even *see* it, and she squeezed her eyes shut and swam on. No elegant torpedo now—she advanced in jerking, uneven fits and starts. *This is not possible,* she told herself when the drag of the crate seemed too much and she could no longer hear Zoose's shouts of encouragement over the pounding of her own heart. *This is not possible,* her mind repeated as she grew weaker and weaker. At last only the word *possible* remained, echoing over and over in her ears: *possible, possible, possible . . .* and then her feet touched rock.

She gave one mighty heave forward and collapsed into the surf. She barely had the strength to look behind her and see Zoose leap off the crate and slog through the water. He yanked at the rope that now cut into her shoulder and chest, slapping her face with his paws and roaring at her to get up. Dimly Freya understood that if she didn't do as he said, the waves would pull her and her cargo back from the beach, where the ocean would claim her once and for all. And so, summoning her last ounce of will, she rose to her feet and hauled the crate ashore.

᠊ᢛ Thirteen ᢛ᠊

*N*ever *stay longer in the water than common sense dictates! Fatigue or chilliness should be a signal for coming out at once!* chided Mrs. Davidson. This intelligence (which likewise appeared in the chapter on Sea-Bathing, after Sandwich Boxes and before Soiled Linen Bags) recommended itself to Freya quite audibly. She opened her eyes. Had Mrs. Davidson descended from on high to scold Freya in person? Yes, there she stood, short yet formidable in a gray serge bathing dress.

"How right you are, Mrs. Davidson. I don't know what I was thinking," said Freya from where she had crumpled to the ground. "Next time I'll try to be sensible."

"No need to be rude! My only aim is to help," said the phantasm reproachfully.

Freya waved the lady away and sat up, struggling to remove the ropes, which had half-dried, half-frozen themselves to her feathers.

"Let me help," offered Zoose from the spot Mrs. Davidson had just vacated. He reached toward her and worked on a knot until it came loose. "Freya, there's bad news," he said, pulling the harness over her head.

His voice sounded strange. Freya waited for him to continue. "The humans landed before we did," he said, fumbling for the right words. "But Death got here first. He was expecting them. He took Knut."

"Oh, no!" cried Freya. She'd always been partial to Knut, with his playful antics and willing nature. "Not after all that. No!"

"Yes," Zoose said. "He did the lion's share of the rowing, but the captain said his heart was weak from getting wet and frozen. Death had his eye on him from the very beginning, I bet. Snatched him right up."

"I want to see him. Can you take me?" asked Freya.

Zoose nodded, and together they picked their way over the rocks and tide pools until they were close to the place where the men had pulled their boat out of the water. They hid themselves behind a dirty chunk of ice and watched the captain make what indentation he could in the hard ground with an ax. Nils crouched near the body of his comrade, his face as blank as the white Arctic sky. When the improvised grave was a few inches deep, the captain and Nils laid Knut within it and mournfully covered him with large flat rocks.

"Zoose," said Freya, "I am going to say the words of a poem. Death has done his business here. I'm sure he's gone. I'll be careful not to invite him back."

Zoose gave Freya a wary nod. She took a long breath and began.

"Death has been the end of you,
a real undoing. It came to break
the fragile thread that life spins out,
and what, oh, what, am I to make
of that? Goodbye, you're gone.

But there's another point of view
that says that Death's a guide.
A chaperone is what it is,
an escort to the other side—
the afterlife. And you go on.

And I go on, although I'd rather not.
My world is dark—you were my sun,
the star that dies at end of day
and disappears, but isn't done.
The dark is real. And so's the dawn."

After many moments of respectful silence, Freya and Zoose wended their way back to the crate.

"You made that one up, didn't you?" said Zoose, guessing correctly. He looked apprehensive but also curious. "What's it mean, that the sun disappears, but isn't done?"

"I'm suggesting that the sun still exists, whether or not we can see it. Knut seems to have gone away, but maybe he's simply in a place where we can't see him," explained Freya, stepping over a pile of sea-worn stones.

Zoose pondered this. "Like a place where only Death can take you? Do you really think so?"

"Goodness, I have no idea whatsoever," Freya said. "But I'd like to believe it. After all, this island is a real place, but you and I never saw it until today. That doesn't mean it didn't exist."

"But it did exist—it was on the map," Zoose pointed out. "Plus, the humans spotted it through their telescope!"

"Indeed they did. But you and I had to take their word for it, didn't we?" said Freya.

Now they were back where they'd come ashore. Freya found that she was famished, and she ate the entire tin of gingersnaps that Zoose had managed to fit in with their things. Then they located a well-hidden patch of sand within the crevice of a rock, and they pitched the silk tent. As for the crate itself, they dragged it back down to the water and let it float away, hoping it would wash up someplace where the humans would find it and make use of it.

White Island was nearly as barren as a meteorite, craggy and almost completely covered with ice. Nevertheless, there were life-forms on it that Freya and Zoose were quick to discover. For one thing, curious little shrimp colonized the frigid pools of water left when the tide went out. Freya used a handkerchief as a sort of net to snare them, and when left to dry for a day or two, she found, they could be made into a nutritious paste that had a buttery, briny flavor. Zoose was crazy for it.

There was also a low-lying shrub that, though hard to find and not much to look at, yielded a dark purple berry. Freya scoured the island for the berries, and whenever she accumulated a sufficient quantity, she pressed them into a juice that she stored in every possible container. With time, she hoped it would acquire the warmth-inducing robustness of Mother's elderberry wine, which she had never quite forgotten.

As before, their chief form of entertainment when they were not gathering food was watching the two remaining humans. Captain Andrée and Nils occupied themselves mainly with collecting driftwood and piling it around their camp, speaking in anxious tones about overwintering on the island. They moved slowly, conserving their strength to better withstand the months to come. Occasionally, Nils sat in the empty boat, addressing the gold locket he still wore around his neck, using many terms of endearment and polishing it with the edge of his scarf. At these times, Captain Andrée kept his distance or went hunting.

One afternoon, the captain shot another walrus, which Nils skinned.

"I don't mind walrus liver," remarked Zoose, for the men wouldn't eat walrus liver any more than bear liver. "Nice and fatty, it is! What I wouldn't give to spread some on a piece of toast!"

"Look at you," Freya said good-naturedly. "I do believe you're rounder in the tummy now than when I met you!"

Zoose patted his belly happily, taking her observation for the compliment it was. "I'm doing all right. You're the clever one with our food. I never would have thought to use a safety pin as a hook for catching fish." It so happened that the small white fish in the shoal waters not far from their tent liked liver as much as Zoose did, and Freya used it as bait.

"Oh, I wish you could try some of the sorrel that used to grow behind my parents' home," reminisced Freya. "It tasted like tart green apples. We made a soup with it that would bring you to your knees."

"I do love a good, hot soup," agreed Zoose eagerly. "Did you ever float oyster crackers in beef broth, and then get them stuck to the roof of your mouth . . . ?" Reconstructing the sumptuous meals of days gone by was another favorite diversion, and so transported did they become that they were no longer on the island, but in some enchanted wonderland where the streams flowed with raspberry syrup, and butterscotch candy dotted the grass like dandelions. And thus for the second time they failed to notice the approach of a polar bear.

It was probably the aroma of fresh walrus blood that drew the bear to the humans' campsite. The walrus was a much more attractive prize than Nils, who looked and smelled nothing like what the bear thought of as food. But from the bear's point of view, Nils was standing between him and his next meal, and that is never a good place for a person to be. The captain heard Nils's cries for help and loaded his rifle as fast as he could, but he was too late. Polar bears are unbelievably strong, and it was over very quickly. Nils lay motionless in the snow, and the bear ambled away, having decided that the walrus was too much trouble after all.

Freya and Zoose were stricken with horror, but the worst part was watching the captain's mind come unhinged. "I shall go mad!" he wailed as he buried Nils in a shallow, rock-covered grave. "Stark raving mad!" he howled into the wind, which muffled his words and blew them away.

"I think he *has* gone mad," said Zoose a few days later as they watched the captain stare into the fog that surrounded the island like a blanket, hour after hour. He rolled up his maps and never touched them again. He stopped eating. His clothes hung from his body in great folds, as though there were nothing inside. "He's almost not even here anymore. He's turning into a ghost."

"Yes, but he's our ghost," said Freya. "He brought us this far, even if he never knew it. Now we can stay with him until the end."

"Until the end?" asked Zoose. "You mean . . ."

Freya nodded. "I think Death will come for him very soon."

She was right, of course. But while the captain waited for Death, the animals made sure he was never alone. During the long nights (which in the Arctic become longer and longer until the sun hardly makes an appearance at all), Zoose fed his fire with pieces of driftwood, never letting it go out. And Freya sat with him while he slept, singing every lullaby she knew and making up a few more. There was no indication that he heard her, but she felt that lullabies were the best defense against nightmares, and she was determined that at least his dreams would be peaceful.

One morning, Captain Andrée went down to the water's edge and shaved his chin. He trimmed his mustache, which was still as blond and admirable as the day Freya first saw him. He tucked his journal, in which he had noted his observations, scientific and personal, into his front pocket and buttoned his coat. Then he sat with his back against an outcropping of rocks, laid his rifle across his lap, and closed his eyes for the last time. Freya and Zoose kept vigil until his final breath.

⚜

"You know," said the mouse, "it wasn't a bad way to go. Death met him in the middle, so to speak." It was springtime. He and Freya had endured their first winter on the island with true grit and were now enjoying the later evenings. They sipped wine by their own fire, which was a direct descendant of the captain's and which they tended as carefully as a garden.

"What are you trying to say?" asked Freya, casting some dry seaweed into the flames.

"I mean, Death didn't overtake him, and the captain didn't try to run away. Seems like they had an appointment with each other, and they kept it," Zoose said.

"Good heavens, for someone who almost fainted the first time I said the word *death,* now you can hardly stop talking about it." Freya laughed.

"I've come a long way," said Zoose with a wink. "And I wonder how much further I'll go. What do you think, Freya? Is this the end of the line for us?"

Freya cocked her head, tossing her yellow feathers a bit. "I suppose we could put up a flag and hope that a whaler might see us."

"Or a whale!" responded Zoose, and they both laughed at that. From time to time they relived their encounter with the whale and the fox, always quoting Marguerite's dubious prophecy that they would miss her, and always surprised that they did.

"Maybe we should build ourselves a hot-air balloon!" said Freya. This was far from the first time she and Zoose had mulled over ways to leave the island, and they took inordinate satisfaction in planning their future exploits. "Did you know, Zoose, that there are mountains in Nepal just waiting to be scaled?"

"You'd have to be off your nut to try something like that," said Zoose. Now it was his turn to poke the fire with a stick and throw on a piece of driftwood, which he did with a practiced flick of his wrist. He wore a spare sock he'd found among the crew's things, wrapping it around himself like a shawl.

"Missing your old sock, are you?" Freya was in a teasing mood.

"A little, maybe," admitted Zoose. "How about you? Do you miss anything? Do you miss home?"

"I am home," said Freya, and poured some more wine into Zoose's cup.

The END

⌘ Afterword ⌘

After months and even years of living together convivially, Freya and Zoose knew each other's brains inside and out. With an icicle, Zoose could trace the streets of Freya's Swedish village into the snow with an easy familiarity, including the back alleys. And Freya could rattle off the names of Zoose's nearly two hundred siblings more fluently than Zoose himself!

"But seriously, Vincenzo-Againzo?" she queried.

"Let's be fair," said Zoose. "Vincenzo's the only name Ma used twice. Of course, they both went by Vinny, so we never knew who was who."

⌘⌘⌘

What was even more interesting was the way in which Freya transferred her knowledge of Mrs. Davidson's *Hints to Lady Travellers* to Zoose. There came a day when Zoose knew every word of it, forward and backward and sideways. He regularly amused himself by inserting nuggets of Mrs. Davidson's wisdom into casual conversation.

"We must bear in mind the proverbial philosophy which tells us that accidents will happen," he intoned as Freya tripped over a rocky crevasse.

"Still, one wonders why they happen so regularly to *me*," replied Freya gamely.

"Damp sheets surely need no preaching against—everyone knows their deadly effects!" cautioned Zoose as they aired out Freya's sleeping bag.

"Frozen sheets are a thousand times worse," Freya quipped.

"Two thousand times worse, even!" agreed Zoose. "And speaking of books—"

"We weren't speaking of books," interrupted Freya.

"Speaking of books," continued Zoose, "wouldn't you agree that 'as a rule, deep or profound reading is not suited to the requirements of travel'?"

"Deep reading!" said Freya. The books they had at their disposal amounted to exactly none. "I'd read the label off a jar of pickles at this point, with relish! Did you hear that, Zoose? I've indulged in a pun!"

"So you did! Well done! And while we're on the subject of food, I insist that 'sandwiches may be eaten, provided they are not of ham,'" quoted Zoose.

Freya groaned. "I'd clobber a ham sandwich right now," she declared. "Why, I'd eat a sandwich made of cardboard and glue if I could get my flippers on one."

"Can we at least agree," Zoose giggled, with a ludicrous affectation, "that 'as fellow passengers, young babies are about as trying as any'?"

Now it was Freya's turn to laugh. "Really, Zoose? Have you ever traveled with a mouse?"

⁂

Another extraordinary development was Zoose's eventual embrace of poetry. Freya was happy to recite every last poem she knew. And she composed original ones weekly to keep up with his growing fondness for verse. The tables were delightfully turned the day Zoose announced that he had invented a poem of his very own.

"It's what you'd call a limerick," said Zoose.

"Oh, is it?" asked Freya.

"Yeah, on account of the syllables," he clarified. "I'm calling it 'The Mouse and the Greeble.'"

Freya was bemused. "Greeble? What's a greeble?"

"Now, look, do you want to hear it or not?" Zoose was nervous, as one often is when sharing a new poem.

"Sorry," Freya said. "Carry on."

"Right. It goes like this," said Zoose.

> There once was a mouse and a greeble,
>
> One was good, and the other pure eeble.
>
> Then a hot-air balloon
>
> Bunged them both to the moon,
>
> Where they jigged for the rest of their meeble.

Freya rolled the words around in her head. She repeated the lines silently, approaching possible interpretations from all the angles. She didn't wish to quash Zoose's zeal. It was, after all, his first attempt. Nevertheless, something about the poem made her feel defensive.

"Everyone enjoys a nice limerick, now and again," she allowed. "And your poem scans very well, despite a few words that I'm fairly certain don't exist, you understand, in an actual language. . . ."

"Artistic liberty," explained Zoose.

"Yes, of course," Freya conceded. "But . . . but . . . was it about *us*? Because it seems that in some non-literal sense you've called me both a 'greeble' and 'pure eeble.' Which is, I have to say, rather hard to know how to take."

Zoose sighed heavily. "Oh, Freya. I had the worst time trying to rhyme 'penguin' with 'wonderfully beautiful.' Went at it every which way, but no dice. Had to invent a few words to get the job done. You can do that in a poem, can't you? Make words up?"

Freya looked at the ground, clearing a small area with her boot as if she had lost something and was trying very hard to find it in the ice and gravel. She adjusted her scarf and smoothed a few of her yellow feathers.

"Make words up?" she repeated at last. "Yes, you can do that in a poem. You can make up all the words you like, Zoose. I'd say you have a gift for it."

~ Author's Note ~

To my readers who are enthralled by Arctic exploration, you will probably recognize the names of the brave men who tried to fly a hydrogen balloon to the North Pole in 1897. Salomon Andrée, Nils Strindberg, and Knut Fraenkel are still regarded as heroes in Sweden, and the country mourned when they failed to return from their great adventure. The country mourned again when, thirty-three years later, their remains were discovered on White Island by a Norwegian sealing expedition, and they were brought home at last.

Salomon Andrée was an engineer who was fascinated by aerial navigation—that is to say, travel by hot-air balloon. His interest was so keen that he determined never to marry, in case his wife ever asked him to stop flying. It's fair to say that he was not a terribly experienced navigator. His balloon trips amounted to a grand total of nine before he attempted a trip to the North Pole. But he was smart and inventive and very determined.

Thanks to Nils Strindberg, the second member of the expedition, we have ninety-three photographs of the doomed voyage. Nils, a physics professor, was very much in love with his fiancée, Anna Charlier, whose picture he carried in a locket. For Anna's part, her last wish (granted, by the way!) was that after her death in England many years later, her heart be removed from her body and buried in Stockholm next to his grave.

Although Knut Fraenkel was several years older than Nils, Freya might be forgiven for mistaking him for the team's youngest member. He was athletic and lively—as a student, his favorite class had been gymnastics! He had no Arctic experience, but he loved to climb mountains and was also a civil engineer. He kept such good meteorological records that we are able to reconstruct the men's journey over the ice quite accurately.

Each human had his own reasons for attempting to reach the North Pole by balloon. We can only guess what those reasons were, but they surely included an ambition to set foot on an entirely unknown place, and the yearning for adventure. In other words, the men were not so different from Freya and Zoose!

⁓✕✕⁓

You might wonder what sort of penguin Freya was, to be small enough to hide away in a basket so success-fully. After all, these birds can grow to be four feet tall, as in the case of the mighty emperor pen-guin! Freya was of a completely different, and much smaller, species; she was a rockhopper pen-guin, and a short one at that. (If you've ever seen a rockhopper penguin, then you know all about their beautiful yellow feathers and orange beaks and bright red eyes.) Here's another fact about "real" rockhoppers: they live in the Southern Hemisphere! You certainly won't find many in Denmark, where Freya's family was from. And would a polar bear really attack a penguin? It's pretty unlikely, since polar bears live in the Northern Hemisphere!

Putting a penguin and a polar bear on the same ice floe is what we call artistic license. Zoose took artistic license when he made up some words for his poem. He and I both sidestepped a few facts in pursuit of a story (or in Zoose's case, a limerick). Frankly, helping oneself to a little artistic license is one of the great perks of being an author. When Marguerite nicked her paw on an icicle, *that* was artistic license! The truth is that arctic foxes, amazingly, have thick fur on the bottom of their feet. They are well protected against snow and ice. (They are also every bit as gorgeous as Marguerite was—no artistic license there.)

Perhaps narwhals are less glamorous than arctic foxes, but they are awe-inspiring creatures. I admit that I didn't know narwhals actually existed until I was in my twenties. I guess I thought they were as imaginary as the unicorns to whom they're forever compared. But no—they're real! Narwhals are wonderfully suited to life in the Arctic Ocean and can dive almost a mile below its icy surface. The tusk of a male narwhal can grow to be ten feet long (I suspect Aarne's was even longer), and once in a very great while, they sprout two of them.

Unlike narwhals, who do best in the cold Arctic Circle, mice find a way to thrive almost everywhere on earth. They are terrific adapters, and in this sense, Zoose was a true mouse. I have no clue what *species* of mouse he was, and neither did he. All I know is that I'm glad he found a friend to help him on his journey. At the end of the day, that was probably more important than the right shoes, or coat, or even cheese.

⸎

There is another player in this cast of characters: the Arctic itself. This ice-covered region has held an enormous allure for explorers hungry to reach the North Pole. The late nineteenth century was awash in men who regarded the "polar dash" as the premier path to glory, both for themselves and their countries. Unfortunately (and dangerously), Arctic sea ice was an insurmountable problem—ships couldn't get through it, and sledges couldn't get across it. That's why flying *over* the ice in a balloon seemed like a marvelous solution to Salomon Andrée! Our planet is warmer now than it was in 1897, and much of the sea ice is melting. Many scientists think that by 2040, it will be possible to sail over an ice-free North Pole.

⚜

I would be remiss if I failed to mention Lillias Campbell Davidson, a veritable patron saint of ladies who desired adventure at the turn of the century! Freya was not the only female to fall under the spell of her book *Hints to Lady Travellers at Home and Abroad*. We shall never know how many voyages were undertaken at Davidson's (very opinionated) urging, nor how many foot warmers purchased, nor how many stern remonstrances given. Small wonder that Freya and Zoose followed her sound advice regarding comfortable cushions! Davidson also wrote an influential guidebook for "lady cyclists" at a time when women were routinely described as physically unfit to mount a bicycle.

Freya & Zoose is both an ode to friendship and a tribute to pioneers of every stripe who yearn for "one true adventure"!

ᴄᴄ Acknowledgments ᴄᴄ

To start at the very beginning, I'd like to thank Don and Ellen Holsinger, who happen to be my parents. They made sure there was a great abundance of books in all the houses we ever lived in, and bankrolled my book-buying sprees in grade school. That early pride of ownership went very deep, and I still feel it!

Thank you, also, to the librarians at Eagle Public Library in Idaho, where I used to take my young children. They placed their staff picks (covers facing outward) on the shelves by the entrance, and I invariably grabbed a few on my way into the building. One of these books was Alec Wilkinson's *The Ice Balloon*, which I read fast and furiously. That week I conceived the idea of a small penguin hiding herself in the basket of a hot-air balloon, and thus Freya was born.

I am grateful to my agent, Steven Chudney. He got behind Freya, Zoose, and their accidental friendship in a big way. That meant quite a lot to me, and still does. In the same vein, Phoebe Yeh gave this book the kind of rigorous, intelligent attention that made it better and better and better. I'm deeply indebted to her and her team at Crown.

David, my husband, has a profound love of reading and writing. It would be ridiculous to try to do any of this without his unstinting support and example. Thank you, David.

Finally, to my own children, who were so interested in the adventures of Freya and Zoose, I write books that I think you will cherish. Everyone has reasons for doing what they do; you are mine.

∼ About the Author ∼

Emily Butler is the eldest of seven children and grew up hiding behind the sofa so that she could read her books in peace and quiet. (It was never quiet.) She finished high school in Brazil, worked on a kibbutz in Israel, practiced law in New York City, catered weddings in London—and was never without a book in her backpack or briefcase. Emily recently moved to Utah with her husband. They live in an old house that is stuffed to the gills with three lovely but disobedient children, and every sort of book.